# WHY I WENT BACK

JAMES CLAMMER

ANDERSEN PRESS

First published in 2016 by
Andersen Press Limited
20 Vauxhall Bridge Road
London SW1V 2SA
www.andersenpress.co.uk

2 4 6 8 10 9 7 5 3 1



British Library Cataloguing in Publication Data available.

ISBN 978 1 78344 377 2

Typeset in Garamond Pro by Palimpsest Book Production Ltd, Falkirk, Stirlingshire

Printed and bound by CPI Group (UK) Ltd, Croydon, CR0 4YY

For Katie

# 1

If you know anyone who knows anyone who wants to find out about magic – specifically whether it's true or not – then send them along to me, because I can tell them for sure.

I'm not talking old-fashioned stuff like rabbits out of hats or sawing the lady in half, which is so historical by now it's practically written into those same books that go on about fat old Queen Victoria in black. And I don't mean the modern stuff either, like you see on TV, where a man with a sharp suit and a beard hypnotises a bunch of builders into dressing up as women or something stupid like that.

That isn't what I'm talking about. Not at all.

Crazy, scary, ancient magic. That's what I mean. The sort of thing that if you came across it for real you'd suffocate and almost fall down with fear right deep in your deepest core and no way, no way, would you ever brush it off or forget about it. And then pretty soon it would get so big inside that you'd have to tell someone about it, get it off your chest, as they say.

That's one of the reasons why I'm writing this down as a story, from beginning to end.

Another is so I can come back in six months' or a year's time and check my head against this account, which is 100% true by the way with nothing added and nothing taken away. I know for sure, now, that I'm different from Mum, who has this whole parallel universe going on inside her head, things that never happened and people that never existed. I know, now, that my feet are planted forever in the mud and the puddles and everything. But sometimes it's good to have proof, separately-existing proof.

Maybe you don't know anyone who's interested in magic. Maybe you're not even that bothered yourself. Feel free to bail out now, if that's the case. Stop reading, do something else instead. Only I don't think you will. Because it's the one thing everybody's interested in, right? Everybody wants *confirmation.*

And that's exactly what I can give you.

You want to hear the story?

Go.

# 2

It starts in the dark, in winter, with a click and a chase.

There I was, standing half-dressed and frozen solid in the middle of my bedroom, the warm square of bed behind me and the black square of window in front dribbling winter rain. I always pulled the curtain back without turning the light on because, first, I wanted to see what the weather was doing and it was easier to see in the darkness and, second, I didn't want to draw attention to myself – every other house and the whole wide world, it seemed, being wrapped snug and slumbering in the black night.

4.16, the red lights of the digital clock said. It was a regular thing, being up at this hour. How long since I'd been doing it? Two weeks? Three? Not that I liked it. I hated it. God how I hated it. I wanted to be back in that warm bed, hands between my legs, dreaming of girls like any normal fourteen-year-old boy should be.

I should probably introduce myself. I may not be the best student at St Stephen's (in fact most people think I'm a bit of a bully, which I'm happy to let them go on thinking) but I've read a few books on the sly and I know that about here's the time you Get To Meet The Main Character. You know the routine – what colour their eyes are and the shape of their nose and what size shoes they wear and all about their brothers and sisters and everything. Well, I don't have any brothers or sisters, and all that other stuff can wait, because *I'm* the main character and I'm real and more than just a shoe size.

Aidan Hale, that's my name, and if you want to know what I look like, all I can think to say is that once I heard a friend of Dad's describing me as a *skinny streak of piss*. So that gives you an idea, even if my skin isn't really yellow. And if you want to know the reason I was up at stupid o'clock, it's because I was going out to work. Just then I was working six days a week and I would have worked seven if I could've got away with it.

Or at least I was, until that *click*.

Someone was lifting the latch on the passageway gate, the brickwork passage that joins our house to next door.

Someone was coming in.

I pressed my face to the rain-dribbled windowpane, cowling my hands round to stop any reflection. The moon showed a little of its light through waste-water clouds. Out in the street a dark shape slouched by a lamppost. The slouch told you straight off that the shape was a he, and that the he was a teenager. Not too big. I felt pretty certain I could have him if it came to a fight.

Trouble was, he had a mate. And one second later the mate's coming out from under *our* passageway, wheeling *my* bike with him. A lighter flared, cupped close in a hand that looked like a pink fleshy flower, as he hitched the bike past the clicking closing gate. The mate was quite a bit bigger than the slouching teenager. I noticed that right away. I'm always sizing people up and reckoning my chances – girls *and* boys (for different reasons of course). It's like an automatic thing with me. Maybe everyone does it, I don't know.

My bike. So what, you're asking? A bike's a bike. They break, or you grow out of them, and then you get another one. Don't you?

Not here. For a start it was brand new, almost. The Pacific Blue frame, the eighteen Shimano gears, the back suspension I'd spent ages adjusting. We didn't exactly have what those English literature writers in the classroom would call a *surfeit of funds*, which meant having anything new was special, something you wanted to hold onto. Mum had never worked because of what went on inside her head. Take where she was just then for example. It wasn't the first place the JobCentre went to when they had a vacancy, put it that way. And as for Dad – Dad was just a postman, and they don't bring in so much money even with overtime, which he hadn't done in years.

In fact (if you want to know the truth, which I've promised to tell) Dad had pretty much stopped being a postman at all, and that was why I needed the bike. Not because it was new, not really, but because without it how was I going to transport the Big Bag, the one hidden downstairs with its piles of letters already sorted into street and house order?

I watched them give the bike a quick lookover by the wet light of the streetlamp. They weren't stupid, you could tell from their body language they were scared and wanted to get out of there as fast as possible but still they couldn't resist having a quick gloat over what they'd plundered. One of them said something and they both laughed without making a noise and that was when every part of my head started *clanging*. It was like all the veins feeding my heart and kidneys etc had short-circuited so that every last bit of blood was slamming into my eardrums instead. Those scumbags. My bike. How could they? How had they even known it was there? I *needed* that bike. I needed it to stop all the bad things that were happening to us from getting any worse.

I heard the wheels ticking softly in the black night. They were on the road. They were going, leaving. And suddenly I couldn't believe it, how I'd been standing there like I was in a trance or something, looking down at them stealing from me without doing a single thing about it. Somehow it had been too easy to watch, a scene from a film almost, what with them in the light of the lamp and me in the dark and the bedroom window between us like a screen at the multiplex.

Dressed in three maybe four seconds. I didn't bother with the outdoor gear, the big coat, the waterproof trousers. The rain wasn't as bad tonight and anyway that stuff rustled and I knew I needed to be silent. Jeans, jumper, trainers and out of the house. I was well practised at that. Dad was fast asleep as usual. It took a lot to get him out of bed these days, what with all the sleeping pills the doctor was giving him.

Down the stairs, easing the door shut behind me. Past the place where I kept the Big Bag hidden with its pre-sorted letters and packets. I thought then, the way you think through a whole complicated situation in a split second, about everything that had happened in those three weeks. The black mornings stealing out of the house, pushing the bike from the passageway. Coasting off through the dead streets praying not to see a single person till it was time to turn round and come home. The terrible Thursday night that had started it all, Mum bent up in a corner, not responding even when you poked or prodded her, and the house filling up with police and paramedics and the woman with the careful deep voice who'd called herself a doctor, the woman who'd signed the papers.

Mum got sectioned, see.

Not everyone knows what that is. If you don't, count yourself lucky.

I turned down the road the teenagers had taken. I had to move fast if I wasn't to lose sight of them. The rain was coming down harder than I'd thought. I started to run, silent and accurate on the slick streets. I didn't care any more how big the second one was. When I caught up with them they'd both be dead and that was a fact.

# 3

Pretty soon all that running'd got me pumped up. They'd *both* got bikes, this pair of scumbags. At first it didn't matter. Once they'd got away from the Immediate Vicinity they were casual as anything, larking about, looping in circles, the one riding my bike, the Pacific Blue, wobbling on purpose like it was too difficult to control. They were going somewhere but it didn't seem to matter much when they arrived. Easy enough for me to get close and jump them when neither was expecting it. Then I made a noise – I must have made a noise though I don't remember doing it. Maybe my trainer splashed in a puddle or something. All at once they were alert, bristling, like those gazelles you see on David Attenborough when they know a lion's onto them. And then the chase really began.

I'm OK at running. They asked me to represent the school one time but then old Sandifer called me into his office once too often and I told him I didn't give a monkey's nuts about it any more. The thing with running is the rhythm. You can't speed up and speed up and expect to sustain it. And suddenly I needed to get turbo-charged and stay there because that scumbag pair were streaking away like the cops were about to get them in a headlock.

I needed that bike. Worst case scenario, *any* bike. I couldn't lose that race.

The streets flew around me – the orange streetlamps and the rising and falling kerbs and the rain everywhere. I never ran like that before in my life. The weird thing was it was almost like I was looking at someone else running and not doing it myself. I had this idea (don't laugh) that if you took a film of me from above, tearing through the streets, and turned me into a dot instead of a person then I'd look like one of those particles whizzing round the Large Hadron Collider in Switzerland or wherever it is. Anyway I was keeping them in sight and I'd already guessed where they were headed. There was a turning at a roundabout – no cars around at that time of night of course – and once I saw them take it I knew for sure. Not that I slowed down. Everything in my head was blurring and if I'm honest I was getting a buzz from that ultra-high level of exercise and what you might call the Righteousness Of My Anger. It was like all the walls between the compartments or boxes in my brain were dissolving, becoming one long landscape instead.

Next thing, I was standing somewhere on the old industrial estate, holding this brick I'd scooped from a pile of rubbish, ready to use it on whoever next popped up in front of my face.

But I'd lost them – or they'd lost me – in the maze of buildings.

I looked at the brick. I listened to my chest and my heart, the invincible muscle-bag that always pumps you from past to future. Both sounded about ready to go into orbit. Puffing hard, I slid into a patch of scrubby shadow next to a derelict warehouse.

Silence all around. A bird soared, black against grey rain-clouds. Where was he going, so high up there?

I thought about what it would mean for me if I really did smash someone with that brick. What it would mean for what the teachers at school liked to call my Long Term Future.

I nestled the brick into a stack of sodden weeds, shuddered out a long soundless breath, decided to try using my brain instead.

The industrial estate. I looked around, as well as I could in the dark and the rain. A few of the buildings here were still in use but most were abandoned places where people never went, secret spaces filled with weird-looking machinery and mountains of broken glass and rotten timber. There were about a million places to hide but only one road in and out. From where I was standing in that scrubby bit of shadow I could see the road, so I knew the scumbag twins hadn't used it to escape. They *might* have dumped the bikes and gone across the wet fields but somehow that didn't feel like their style.

They were here somewhere. All I had to do was listen and watch and wait for them to give themselves away.

It happened almost immediately.

# 4

The voices were low, urgent, worried.

I slipped through the shadows, trying to locate them. Which direction? Far edge of the estate. My legs felt shaky now I'd stopped running. I knew I wouldn't be able to chase them if they got away a second time.

Take it easy. Watch where you're putting your feet. Keep your breathing under control. Act like someone from one of those old-time movies, escaping the Germans.

The moon had gone for good, lost behind bottled up cloud. Turning a corner into a sodden overgrown alley I saw, at the far end, the glowing tip of a cigarette. A match flared and another tip joined it.

Then another.

'. . . believe you did that. *And* letting someone follow you.'

'There wasn't anyone, Christy, promise.'

'Well, was there or wasn't there?'

'I don't know, we just thought that – hey!'

One of the red cigarette tips flew sideways and dropped out of sight.

'Idiot!'

I went closer, zigzagging in slow motion, testing each step for stones or sticks or anything that might make a noise, watching as I brushed against a bush and a thousand raindrops exploded silent against my shoulder.

'What are you, some kind of retard? Don't you remember what we agreed? And then you go out nicking bikes!'

'Sorry, Christy . . .'

'And you should have stopped him, Deano. I mean, it's not like you're *unknown* or anything . . .'

'Just having a laugh, that's all it was.'

'For this piece of crap?' Something clattered in the darkness and I knew it was the Pacific Blue being kicked to the ground. Whoever Christy was (they said it so it sounded like *crispy*), he wasn't making much of an effort to keep quiet. His voice sounded odd and scratchy, like his throat was full of salt and scabs. 'We don't do this any more. Not since – *that*.' A burning cigarette tip stabbed back and forth, indicating the building behind them. 'Let's get this sorted right now. Were you followed or not?'

'No . . .'

'Deano?'

'No. Definitely not. William here was imagining it.'

'William Here!' Christy said. 'William Here would probably hand over the *key*!'

'I wouldn't!' protested William Here.

'Barney and Lee are in there with him. They reckon he's asleep but I think he's pretending. We need to get back and check on them. Bring the fags with you. And bring that crappy bike! The last thing we want is someone finding it and getting interested in how it ended up here.'

A door opened in the building, black against black, and the three of them disappeared inside, dragging the Pacific Blue behind them like a piece of junk.

# 5

So that was that. The silence came down again, a great damp blanket you could never push back up. The blanket sagged right down over my heart and for a while I stood there doing nothing and thinking nothing. Then I counted the names I'd heard. Five. The scumbag twins had turned into quintuplets. And they'd done so much damage to my bike what with all that dragging and kicking that it was probably wrecked, or soon would be.

I couldn't fight five of them, even supposing I *could* get inside that big black building. Christy just on his own sounded like a nutjob. As for the talk of keys and someone pretending to be asleep, well, I didn't give a rat's arse about any of that. I hardly even realised I'd heard it till afterwards, so fixated was I on that bike.

Minutes passed while I wondered what to do next.

An enormous spread of rusted wire stood close by, grown

through with weeds and bushes. It was big solid wire, too thick to bounce around. I pushed my way through to a tiny space in the middle. It smelt of animals and stagnant water but I didn't care about that. Nobody would see me there unless they shone a torch directly in and I couldn't imagine Christy or Deano or William Here having one of those.

I thought about the Big Bag at home, the letters and packets still waiting to be delivered.

None of them would be going out today.

Maybe the Pacific Blue wasn't so badly damaged. It *was* new, after all. Well-made. A quality product. Maybe I'd be able to fix it up, if I could get my hands on it.

Those people inside – those teenagers – they had to leave sometime. Didn't they have homes or schools, or jobs even, to go to?

That thought decided me. What else was I going to do anyway? I'd wait till the whole bloody lot of them pissed off and then find a way to break in. Smash a window if I had to, it wouldn't be the first time. Most of them round there had reinforcing wire but if you went at them hard enough you could get through fine. Once inside I'd find my bike and get out. It was obvious they couldn't care less about it. Maybe it was lying forgotten already. If all that was too dangerous in the dark, I'd wait for dawn.

Easy.

I settled down, pulling my jumper up over my head and down over my knees, trying to stretch it in both directions. I was soaked right through by now and shivering but at least the wire and the bushes were keeping the worst of the rain off. The jumper was one of those Mum had knitted from a pattern. Normally I didn't wear it, but it was the first thing my hand grabbed for when the chase began. I looked down at it and wondered what Mum would say, me ruining something she'd made so slowly and so carefully. Then I reminded myself how Mum wasn't thinking about jumpers any more. There were a lot of things she wasn't thinking about any more, and a whole lot of new things she couldn't stop thinking about.

Scary things. Random, impossible things.

Whispers in the schoolyard, always behind my back.

*Aidan's mum's a psycho . . . Aidan's mum's a psycho . . .*

I hated hearing those whispers, because they were right.

# 6

It wasn't long before I was feeling a bit psycho myself. I'd sat there in the middle of that heap of rusted wire for hours, or so it seemed. And that smell. At first it hadn't bothered me. Animal. Fox it must be. White snout, rust-red ears. And somehow I was the one leaping and jumping with a red bushy tail nailed to my arse. Being chased by a shape in the sky, a threatening cloud, something that was about to fall on me like the biggest waterfall you'd ever see. Here it came, slapping me round the face and shoulders. I crouched, threw my arms over my head, tried to protect myself. In the distance a rainbow. Letters and packets whirled about me by the thousand. The Queen's head bulged, fixing me in the eyes, fierce, full of punishment. I tried to shovel the letters into the Big Bag but there were too many. I tried to run but they followed me, fell on top of me, collapsing paper houses and anyhow I couldn't run properly because my feet were changing shape. I tried to speak, to shout for help, but the only sound coming out was a bark and then letters were flying like wasps into my mouth.

My head jerked up.

A van, a white battered-up Ford Transit, was reversing, driving away.

Must've nodded off.

I shuddered away from the familiar sweaty nightmare, yanked my head back into real time. The scumbags had a *van?* How many people inside? More than one in front I reckoned but I couldn't be sure, only caught a glimpse. With vans you never know anyway.

I couldn't wait any longer. I knew that much. I was freezing up, my warmth and energy congealing like sausage grease in a cold frying pan. Even so I forced myself to hang on another couple of minutes before trying the door they'd gone in by. No luck. Shut tight, you couldn't even prise your fingers past the metal tongue welded round its edge. I wasn't getting in that way. I ran round the building searching for other doors, windows, basement entrances, anything. The sky was brightening in one corner. Before the whole thing with Mum started I'd never even seen the dawn, at least not since I was a baby. I don't mean the orange dawn, the nice bit where the sun shows itself, I mean the very first grey streaks that somehow make you feel old inside because you know the only other people seeing it are the sick and the sad and the bloody ancient milkman.

There. Bingo. A ladder going straight up the side of the building, tall weeds tangling the bottom. Fire escape. The metal rungs were like ice in my hands but from the top you could see everything, all the little houses and schools and shops and roads, and standing still for a moment I wondered why I'd never been up there before because looking down on everything like that made you feel you were king of the whole wide world.

In one corner of the flat factory roof there was a sort of hut thing with a door hanging by one hinge.

I pushed it aside. Steps led down.

Pray they were all in that van, driving away. Or at least that nutjob Christy was. He'd sounded like someone who'd get himself behind a steering wheel the minute his legs were long enough, no worries about that.

Pray the place was empty.

Head booming with blood-drums all the same. Think. Where would they put it? Ground floor. Obvious. No point taking it anywhere else.

Leaves on the stairs, feet skidding in mountains of pigeon droppings.

Two minutes later I was on the ground floor, dirty windows letting in just enough light to see by. Everywhere and everything silent like I'd landed on an acre of moon. Piles of rubble lay scattered and the wet winter smell of a forgotten place hung in the air. Massive machines rotted on metal plinths. I went up to one of them. What had it done before the rust came? Chopping or packing or sorting or moulding or cutting. A control box dangled from a cable, three white buttons and one red. The top button said START. I watched my finger press it. Stupid. But nothing happened.

Forget the machines. Beyond them there was a corridor. Offices once, must have been. I stopped, listened. Heard nothing. Very very slowly I opened a door. Dust and rubbish, a turned-over table, a noticeboard with green drawing pins, a faded sign that read *This is a Work Station not a Pigsty So Tidy Up after Yourself.* Next to it, a doorless room stuffed with old-fashioned orange furniture, a filthy works canteen. Three of the four walls had random holes sledgehammered all over them so they looked like gigantic slabs of Swiss cheese.

Next to that, a bit further along, a door secured with a silver hasp and padlock.

The padlock didn't have a key in it and it didn't mean the Pacific Blue was inside but this was the most likely-looking place I'd seen so far. And just that padlock on its own, with its steel-barred U being the only bit of shiny new metal among all that dirt and rust and mould, was enough to get me super-curious.

They must all have been in that van. I felt sure of it now. Nobody locks a room when they're still inside it themselves, do they?

I tapped my fingers along the top of the frame, the first place you should always look. Nothing. I looked around, moving the toe of my wet trainer about in the dirt and rubbish. Something told me the key was nearby, that they hadn't taken it with them. I moved up and down the corridor, looking, feeling. My foot brushed a place where the wall and floor met. A piece of plaster fell away. Behind the plaster something glinted.

I took the key and fitted it to the padlock.

*Click.*

Screw you, Christy. Screw the sodding lot of you.

Inside. A long derelict storeroom. Rectangular windows set high at the far end, their panes mostly smashed by rocks thrown from outside. Clear light coming through, the first clear light for days. Maybe the rainclouds were breaking up at last. One or two of the random sledgehammered holes showed through the breeze block from the canteen next door. Close by, on a pair of wooden pallets that had been arranged side by side, lay a mound of greasy blankets and clothes.

My bike was leaning against the far wall. The Pacific Blue frame, the eighteen Shimano gears, the back suspension I'd spent ages adjusting. Scratched up, kicked about, but looking like it'd still work OK. There was other stuff too, among the beer cans and fag ends at that end of the room – other bikes, games consoles, computers, a washing machine, stuff I hardly bothered glancing at.

I went to get the bike and that was when I saw two white eyes staring at me from inside the pile of blankets.

# 7

He was up in a second, moving forward as if to intercept or stop me and I was moving fast too though I can't tell you in which direction because a tonne of pure distilled fear had suddenly got me speared up and down. I know the muscles in my arms flexed and I know my fists were up and sweat was boiling across the top of my head.

'Please!' he cried out. 'Not again . . .'

'Keep away!' I shouted. 'Don't come any nearer!'

'Let me sleep . . . At least let me sleep . . .'

I must've looked like I was about to beat hell out of the whole wide world what with my hands pulled back like that, stone-hard fist-blocks, because I saw then that what he was really doing was trying to protect himself.

'Keep away,' I warned him again, not dropping the attack position but taking a step closer to the bike – the bike that was propped beyond him.

'Don't,' he rasped. 'Please, don't . . .'

His palms flapped up in a sort of surrender, then he lowered himself back onto the wooden pallets and pulled one of the greasy blankets round his shoulders. I knew by then that he couldn't be much of a threat, old man that he was. His eyes were so pale they hardly seemed to have any pupils. They stared at me in the clean weak light and my own eyes stared right back.

'You're not one of them,' he said after a moment. 'Are you?'

'Look, I don't know what's going on here, but—'

'Want to know? Eh? Want to know?

'I just need that bike, that one over there, see, and then I'm—'

The old man bent and grabbed his ankle and the ankle rattled and chinked. '*That's* what's going on.'

There was a chain, padlocked round so tight that the foot below was coloured up like a plum. Pulling the chain, he showed me how the other end was fastened, again by padlock, onto the wooden pallets.

'I can drag them a yard or so. Then it gets too painful.'

'Jesus.' My fists went down. The pallets were the big heavy kind, full of giant metal staples. 'Haven't you tried to escape?'

I remembered then the scumbags, out in the dark with their glowing cigarette ends, talking about *keys* and someone *pretending to be asleep*.

'Yes. Tried.'

I went closer. Apart from the foot and some purple bruises on his neck and a lot of dried-out yellow hair everything about him was thin and colourless: the cheeks that were scooped out, the eyes that really did seem bleached as if somehow the back of his skull was showing through. He wore cheap sports clothes, a grey Admiral hooded top that reached down almost to his knees, thin tracksuit bottoms, a pair of scuffed-up old Reeboks.

Must be frozen, in this weather.

He settled back into the soft nest he'd made for himself. I saw now there was a dirty cushion for a pillow and even a coverless duvet. That was his bed. There was a bucket too, off to one side, not that I wanted to go anywhere near it.

He gathered the blanket closer round his shoulders and stared at me a bit more.

A bird chirping outside or a cloud passing across the early-morning sun, some new thing, jerked me back into myself just then. It was time to toughen up, time to get back in the centre of my own situation. I'd forgotten the Big Bag, forgotten Mum and how all this with the bike (when it came right down to it) was about her. Whatever was going on here – the stolen stuff, the skinny old guy chained up – it was nothing to do with me. Besides, seeing the chain and the swollen ankle had given me a new appreciation of Christy and his friends. This wasn't ordinary thieving. Holding someone *prisoner*. The poor bloke was half dead from starvation. Bad enough if they had a reason for it. If they *didn't*, if they were doing it just for laughs, then it was sick. Way way beyond what I'd ever got up to at school with bullying and disruption, so-called.

Sooner or later, Christy and his pals would be coming back. I needed to make sure I wasn't there when they did.

I edged past the chained-up man and made a grab for the Pacific Blue.

'I'm going,' I said. 'I'm taking this. And if you tell anyone I've been here then I'll come back and I'll – I'll . . .'

'I understand. Only when they see *that's* gone –' (he nodded towards the bike) – 'they'll know someone's been here.'

'So?'

I was almost at the door when he whispered, 'They'll take it out on me.'

'What?'

'They'll take it out on me. They'll *make* me tell – about you.'

I stopped. I looked down at my hands on the saddle and handlebars. Without those to grip I knew they'd be shaking. To tell the truth they hadn't really stopped since I'd seen his ghostly old eyes watching me from under that pile of blankets. 'They don't know who I am,' I said.

'Of course. Only . . .'

'Only what?'

'If they made me *describe* you . . .'

I stood in the doorway, trying to work it out. This wasn't the kind of calculation they made you do in maths.

The Big Bag. Impossible to do the Big Bag without a bike. And I needed to do it if I wanted to keep Dad at home, keep him visiting Mum and helping her get better. I needed that bike.

Versus –

If the bike was gone, if the man in the blanket told them about me . . .

Deano and William Here knew which house they'd pinched the bike from. If Christy then figured out I'd seen their prisoner . . .

If they were happy locking someone up and starving them, what would they do to me, another teenager?

Those minutes at the end of school, the minutes of jostling escape when anybody and everybody can get at you. A flashing blade out in the road, a lunge nobody notices. A wound in the stomach or side, a body falling to the ground.

Or was I being paranoid? I couldn't work it out. It was like impossible algebra, life-or-death algebra.

And anyway, what *would* they do to this poor guy here?

'I don't believe they'll be back tonight,' he said softly. 'Don't worry. You've time to decide.'

'How do you know I'm deciding anything?'

'Why else would you stop? Not only stopped, but returned. Shows uncertainty.'

He was right. Without realising it I'd drifted back into the room.

'Think you're pretty clever, don't you?'

'Not particularly.'

I said nothing. I looked at him, I looked at my bike. I looked at the other bikes. Maybe I should take one of those, a knocked-about one. That way it couldn't be connected to me. But then there was still the problem of whether or not I could trust blanket-man to keep his mouth shut.

'Did you come in on the back of a lorry?'

'Pardon?'

'My dad, he says you all come in on the backs of lorries. Taking our jobs.'

'No. I didn't come in on the back of a lorry.'

'But you're not from here, are you? I mean, you're not like us, British.'

'What makes you think that?'

'Your accent. It's . . . weird.'

'I'm as British as they come.'

'Look,' I said. 'They nicked my bike and they've got you chained up. We're on the same side, aren't we?'

'You tell me.'

'I mean, that chain – I couldn't break it, never in a million years . . .'

'Suppose not,' the man said miserably.

'What's your name?'

'Haxforth.' He bowed his head. 'At your service.'

I thought about telling him my name then decided No. 'I really need a bike. So I'm going to take one. Not mine, if it'll cause too much trouble. Just an old one, that one hidden at the back there. You got a problem with that?'

He shrugged. 'Every thief for himself.'

I put the Pacific Blue back in its abandoned dusty position and picked my way over to where a beat-up old racing bike stood and hauled it out and made sure it worked OK, brakes and gears and chain. As I wheeled it to the door (Haxforth watching me the whole time) a car soft-roared somewhere in the early-morning silence. The world was coming back to life. Then another one – louder and closer. It probably wasn't Christy and his pals coming back but I didn't want to take the chance. It was time to go. *Way* past time.

'"At your service," you said.'

'That's right.'

'Keep your mouth shut then.'

'Mum's the word.'

'I mean it. Forget I was ever here.'

'Already done.'

Out in the corridor I turned back to look at him. 'What's so important, anyway – that they've got you chained up like that?'

Haxforth pulled the blanket tighter against the morning freeze. 'They think I know how to find something they want. Want badly.'

'What?'

'Sorry.' He smiled grimly. 'I never give anything away for free. Especially information.'

'Suit yourself.' I closed the storeroom door, trying at the same time to shut down that part of my memory where he lived already. Then I locked the padlock and put the key back behind the piece of loose plaster. I really didn't want anyone knowing I'd been there.

I pushed the bike towards the rusting machines on the factory floor.

All I wanted to do right then was get the hell out as fast as I could.

# 8

The school gates, bright blue and bright yellow, the kind of colours they think will make you feel happy. Blue sky above, better. Real. No more clouds. Cold and sunshiny.

The clock – the lopsided clock in Miss Tuckett's classroom window – said 8.20. Almost nobody about. The car park full and all the teachers inside planning the latest tedium. One or two kids kicking around, none I was interested in though.

*He* better get here before I nod off, that's all.

I sat on the low wall by the gates, wanting to think everything that had happened through clear and methodical but the only thing my brain would focus on was the new bike. It might be a bit rusty but it worked fine, brakes and gears and chain. And so *thin*. A racer, not a mountain bike like my proper one. The wheels about the width of my thumb and the saddle so small and sharp I thought it'd cut me when I first sat on it.

First sat on it. When? Two hours ago? Wobbling like I'd never been on a bike before.

It was safe at home now. Locked up and hidden where Dad wouldn't see it. The last thing I wanted was for him to be asking questions about where the Pacific Blue had gone. But there'd been no time for the letters today. No time to clear the Big Bag. Please please please don't let Dad bring home as much today as he did yesterday.

Fat chance, what with Christmas coming.

8.25. Kids arriving now, drifting in. They saw me sitting on the low wall and crossed the path to avoid me. Good. One or two I knew, one or two I'd done in the past but not today. Too tired today.

Thinking how I'd got the bike out of that old factory. There hadn't been any other way but the way I'd come in. Bike on the shoulders, up the stairs, wheeling it onto the flat roof. And then overhead that sudden blue sky. Strange how the clouds had cleared so fast. In that moment I'd felt free of everyone and everything. If only I could find a way of jumping into the blue and never coming down.

Bike on the shoulders, the rungs slippery and cold. One by one by one. Much harder going down than up, you wouldn't think that would you.

Riding away, legs made of marshmallow.

'Here,' said a hesitant voice.

I looked up. 'Morning, stupid,' I said.

'Take it, then.'

'I will. Thanks very much.'

I pocketed the two pound coins while Daniel Cushway looked at me with the same unhappy face I'd seen every day for the past two weeks. Round and pale, with a yellow pus-filled spot on the side of his nose. A face that if it caught you in the wrong mood was asking to be punched.

'That's a beauty, Daniel,' I said, pointing to the spot. 'You want to get your mum to pop that for you.'

'What?' he said. 'Oh yes – yes . . .'

I glanced over my shoulder, wondering if any teachers were watching. Way off in one of the buildings, behind a first-floor window, Mr Eaton was staring out with his arms folded. But he was too far away to see exactly what was going on and anyway I shifted my body to block his view.

'I don't think I can do this tomorrow,' Daniel Cushway said. 'Mum's asking questions. About why I need so much money every day. She's not stupid, she knows how much school dinners cost. She called up the school to check.'

He kind of gulped as he said all this.

I flexed my hands. The stone-hard fist-blocks were coming back, the clanging head. I wanted to smash him in the face right there right then only it was too risky, too public. I wanted to shout at him, What about *my* mum, don't you know what's happening to her, don't you know how she hears voices in her head that drive her crazy and now they've put her in Tredegar House which is only where the worst of the nutters go and they're pumping her full of drugs that're turning her into a zombie and why should I GIVE A TOSS about your mum or her bloody dinner money?

Too risky. Too public.

I smashed him in the face anyway.

Then kids were gathering around and shouting and a whistle was blowing and I saw Mr Eaton flying out of a distant door, charging towards me.

I gazed up into the blue sky and waited for the arms to haul me away.

# 9

'We do our best to accommodate everyone here at St Stephen's, but there are limits beyond which we as a school community cannot go. You know that as well as anyone, Aidan.'

The headmaster's office. Again. The scratchy brown carpet stuffed with static electricity and the framed certificates on the wall and the picture nobody could think was any good.

And the headmaster. Old Mr Sandifer. Red-faced and red-nosed, with a great thick red neck and a poppy in the breast pocket of his suit even though Remembrance Sunday was weeks ago.

'Aidan?'

I didn't say anything, just looked straight past him out the window.

'It always seems to be you, doesn't it? Why is that? Can you give me an answer?'

'Isn't just me, sir.'

'No? Who else then? Daniel Cushway? What exactly is going on between the two of you?'

A long silence till I said, 'Nothing. There's nothing's going on.'

'Is everything OK at home? Any problems?'

I glanced at him. He was leaning back in his chair, steepling his fingers in front of his mouth, staring right at me. Did he know anything about those whispers in the schoolyard?

'If there are, just say and we might be able to help you . . .'

I closed my eyes, tried to shut out the world. Thinking, You don't know *anything* about what's going on at home and you wouldn't understand even if I told you, which I never will.

'Because you're treading a very fine line now. We can't have any more of these distractions. You're extremely fortunate that none of the teachers saw exactly what happened. But let me assure you that another incident like this and I will be contacting your parents, at the very least. I may also have to involve the police and we could be looking at another suspension.'

'It won't happen again,' I said quietly.

I meant it, too. I didn't want the police poking around, because of Dad, because of what Dad was doing.

'Please make sure that it doesn't. You can go to your class now.'

I stood up, feeling the static cling of the carpet. At the door Mr Sandifer asked me to wait and he came over and put a big red hand on my shoulder. 'You know, Aidan, I hate to say it, but there are always people worse off than us. Either of us. Try to give some thought to them.'

'I will,' I said, as the door closed.

I padded along corridors. Through a window I saw steam coming from the boiler room, saw beyond it the new science block someone had tried to burn down last year. I thought what a bad job they'd done, how I'd go about it if it was me. Grey pipes hung overhead, benches and bags and posters on the walls, the white metal bells waiting for their next time to howl. Pens scratched like mice behind doors, teachers talking, kids listening. Kids learning. Learning and listening, smiling and laughing and joining in.

My door. I didn't bother to knock, it'd seem too pathetic. Straight in, straight into history with Miss Tuckett.

Everyone stared at me. Nobody spoke. Down at the front I saw Daniel Cushway with something white, something hygienic, smeared across his mouth. Miss Tuckett coughed like she was embarrassed. She was new and nervous. I walked to the back of the classroom and sat down in my regular seat. I didn't have my books but somebody handed me a pen and a blank piece of paper. I said Thanks then folded my arms flat on the table and put my chin on them.

'Aidan?'

'Yes, miss?'

'Homework. I've got everyone else's.'

'Left it at home, miss.'

'You've had two weeks to do this, Aidan,' she said, trying to sound stern.

I shrugged.

'See me at the end of the lesson.'

'Yes, miss.'

I knew they'd been having meetings about me. I knew she was worried about what I'd do next.

'Now, back to our subject. I asked you all to re-read chapter seven of *The Romans and After*. Has everyone done that? Hands up, please.' Miss Tuckett waddled around, looking to see who had and who hadn't. Mine stayed down and she pretended not to notice.

'Fine. Good. Let's get something up on the board. You should know all this, so let's whizz through it quickly. The Romans. You've spent your whole life living under them, living by their rules, being protected by their armies, and then suddenly they're gone. You don't know why, but they're gone. Everything around you is changing. Let's try to imagine what that was like.' She took a marker pen and wrote on the whiteboard, The Dark Ages.

'Write that down, please. The period after the Romans is often known as the Dark Ages. Why is that? Anyone?'

'Because all the lights went out,' somebody said in a bored voice.

'In a way,' replied Miss Tuckett. 'Although of course there wasn't any electricity at the time. Electricity wasn't invented until the nineteenth century.'

'Discovered,' Daniel Cushway said. 'Electricity wasn't invented, it was discovered.'

I rolled my eyes. He really was an idiot.

'Thank you, Daniel.' Miss Tuckett made an effort to smile. 'But let's stick to the Dark Ages. Now, the Roman army. We know all about them, don't we? It was their discipline that kept them winning on the battlefield, but once they'd invaded a place they acted more like a police force, protecting the towns, guarding the roads and the food supply. So, what would it be like if one day all the police just disappeared. What do you think would happen?'

'There'd be loads of fights,' Gemma Shaw, over by the window, said. 'People'd go round helping themselves to stuff.'

'Good.' Miss Tuckett wrote Breakdown of Law and Order on the whiteboard. 'Copy that down. Anything else?'

'The Roman roads would fall apart,' called out Suzanne Dartnell.

'Excellent.' Miss Tuckett wrote Roads Gone, No Easy Transport on the whiteboard and we copied that down too.

'. . . And if other people tried taking over, there wouldn't be anyone to protect you and you might end up having to be their slave, or even being killed.'

'Thank you, Suzanne. That's right. Especially people from abroad, invaders. And who were the first people to invade Britain after the Romans left?'

'The Vikings?' someone said.

'Actually it was the Anglo-Saxons. The Vikings came later. Although I can think of *several* people here who must have been Vikings in a previous life.'

One or two laughed at that, but not me.

'It still hasn't answered my question, though. OK, yes, life was a lot harder, but that's not really why it was known as the Dark Ages. Any more ideas?' Miss Tuckett looked around the class. 'No? Well, it's because nobody wrote anything down. Or hardly anybody. The Romans loved to write and they had plenty of leisure time in which to do it. So there are lots of different sources and from those we can get a pretty good idea of how they lived. Remember our sources? Important for when it comes to exams.'

Everyone nodded, wrote Sources in their exercise books.

'But after they'd gone, nobody had the time. They were too busy trying to survive to leave records. And remember not very many people could write in the first place, only certain educated members of this new society. OK. So the Dark Ages are called the Dark Ages because we don't know very much about them. To us, here in the twenty-first century, it's a period of darkness. Write that down.'

'Miss?' I said, putting up my arm.

'Yes, Aidan?' Miss Tuckett said warily.

'How do we know anything about them at all then?'

'Good question – although we *did* cover this earlier in the term. Well. There are bits and pieces. We know there were different kingdoms and we have a little of their writing and we know some of their legends. One is a poem called *Beowulf*. In fact, that'll be your homework over Christmas, everyone, to read the translation of *Beowulf* that I'll be handing out at the end of the lesson. I want you to find out what sort of life the person who wrote it might have led.'

Groans.

Miss Tuckett smiled. 'Don't worry, it's not a love poem. It's one for all you invaders out there – about kings and witches and monsters. Believe me, if you lived in the Dark Ages, things like that were just as real as a mobile phone is to you or me today.'

I pushed my chair back and tried to get my head comfortable on flattened arms. It was a double lesson so there was plenty more of this stuff to come. What did I care about things that happened hundreds or thousands of years ago? Loads of it was probably guessing anyway. What I *really* needed was some sleep. That's what school's for. They're happy with that. Let poor old hateful old Aidan Hale go to sleep and leave the rest of us alone to get on with our learning and listening and smiling.

Except it wasn't proper sleep, not like night-time. More like drifting. Thoughts and images going round and round my head. The latch on the gate lifting and falling. Christy talking in the dark, flicking cigarette ash. The door on the factory rooftop hanging open. An old white hand rattling a chain.

*You know, Aidan, there are always people worse off than us. Try to give some thought to them.*

He was right, old Sandifer. I wanted to see Haxforth again.

I needed to find out what was really going on.

# 10

Dad first though.

Knowing how it was going to be before I even opened the door.

TV on, not too loud. Royal Mail coat hanging in the hallway. A bag of chips open on the kitchen table, next to the fruit bowl with the shrivelled apple and the red bill from the gas company. A little polystyrene tub of curry sauce.

The house cold. Midwinter. In half an hour it'd be dark.

'Hi,' I said, jabbing my toe into the place where the carpet was coming away because I had to do something like that and couldn't think what else.

'Hi, Aidan,' he said, not looking up.

'Hi.' I couldn't think of a single other thing to say.

'Watching the game tonight? It's the Arsenal.'

'Might do,' I said, knowing I wouldn't.

'Chips on the table for you. Couple of quid too, dinner money for tomorrow. Sorry I forgot about today.'

'That's all right.'

'They don't let you starve though, do they?'

'No.'

He was slumped back on the brown sofa, boots still on, his best friends a can of lager and the remote control. Curtains closed. This was one of his three places. The other two were the kitchen table for eating and the bed for sleeping. He hadn't had a bath since Mum left. By the light of the TV his face looked green, like a bad chip.

'Did you go to work today?' I asked quietly.

He nodded, only half listening.

I looked out towards the shed, disappearing into the dark. Thinking, What a liar you are. You might have *gone* to work, but did you *do* any work?

'Visiting time'll be over in a couple of hours,' I said.

'I'm not going tonight.' He glanced at me, eyes hooded, not wanting to be seen. 'They said not to. I went yesterday and they said leave it a couple of days, wait till she's over the worst of it.'

'Next time you go, can I come?'

He shifted on the sofa. For a moment I thought he might even stand up. The volume on the TV went down a fraction. 'Look, Aidan, this is going to take time. It's not like getting over a cold . . .'

'I know that,' I said, jabbing my toe harder into the carpet. 'I'm not stupid.'

'Nobody's saying you are.'

'I just want to know what's going on.'

'They've got her in there for assessment. Stabilisation. They're the experts.'

I looked over at the mantelpiece, the two photographs. One

of me as a baby, a pink bundle of do-nothing. The other, Mum and Dad on their wedding day. Dad looking like the cat who's got the cream, and you can see why because Mum is so beautiful. Blonde and young and thin, not like she is now. But even there, even among those wedding-day smiles, there's something in her eyes that says, I don't know exactly what's going on or really who these people are at all.

Dad now, here, watching telly. The cat who lost the cream, whose paw got mangled up instead.

'Watch the football with me,' he said.

'I can't.' I gave the carpet a final kick. 'Got homework to do.'

'Course. Homework's important.'

I went upstairs. Behind me, the volume on the TV edged up.

# 11

Dawn outside the derelict factory. A peeling sign I hadn't noticed before said *Brace Brothers* in swishy-type lettering. No clue about what the Brace Brothers ever did inside.

The Big Bag was empty. It had gone OK today. The old racing bike might look weak but when you got used to it it was fast and light and the brakes were brilliant. No incidents, nobody up and about and asking awkward questions when I poked their letters through. No heavy parcels, no rain. Every door silent and locked against the winter. The start of the Christmas rush. Just about keeping on top of it.

I'd hidden the bike at the roundabout end of the industrial estate. Now I waited and watched, hidden too, in the overgrown alley where I'd eavesdropped on Christy and his pals the night before. The place was dead, no cars, no voices, nothing. Even the ghosts weren't bothering with it this morning.

Easy not to believe in ghosts once the sun's up.

This time I had my torch, and something else too – something I'd taken from the shed at home. How I hated that shed, hated what was in there and what it was making me do. But there were other things inside it as well, regular shed-type things, old hammers and chisels and trowels on dirty shelves, cobwebby tools left behind by the people who'd lived in the house before us, or even from the people before them. I looked at one of them now, the hacksaw I'd snatched from a hook, checked the blade with my thumb. Quite a lot of rust came away. I ignored that though. It felt good having something solid, something metal, in my hands.

Up the ladder, into the sky. Not blue any more but grey on grey. Pushing aside the hanging door on the little rooftop hut. Down the stairs, avoiding the broken glass and the mountains of pigeon droppings. I didn't want to turn the torch on but pretty soon I had to because the gloom was deeper than before. I cupped it in my hands, making a pink fleshy flower.

Every other step stopping and listening and hearing only my heart, the invincible muscle-bag, and the breath locked deep in my lungs.

Was this really such a great idea? I thought of Christy, of how he must have planned this, picking the location, getting the locks and chains, organising Haxforth's imprisonment. All that made me surer than ever that he was somebody I never wanted to meet.

Ground floor. The dead acre of moon once more.

99.9% sure the place was unguarded.

Haxforth. Who was he? *What* was he? The truth was, I was starting to think he hadn't been real at all. An old man locked inside a filthy storeroom, frozen and starved, with bleached-out eyes that looked as if his skull was showing through? It was all too difficult to believe. And really that's why I went back. Because maybe what Mum had I had too and finally it was starting to show itself. See, I'd once heard a doctor say on the radio how schizophrenia was often inherited, and how it often presented first in teenage years (that was how he said it, 'presented', like it was some TV show), and I'd been worrying myself stupid about it ever since.

Mild hallucinations to begin with, this doctor had said. Auditory and visual.

And I was fourteen going on fifteen, which was about as teenagery as it was possible to be.

Past the weird-looking machinery, the dangling control box with its three white buttons and one red.

All I could think of was getting into that room again. And that then I'd see a man with a chain around his ankle and he'd be able to give me some explanation, however shaky, for why he was there. Because if I didn't see him – if the room was empty of everything except beer cans and fag butts – then I reckoned my chances of landing in a mental institution sometime in the near future were pretty high. Maybe they'd put me in a ward next to Mum, and that would be my Glorious Future. The hacksaw I'd brought more as a lucky charm if I'm honest. Proof, almost – cold, hard proof in my hands – that what I'd seen before was real, and so would be real again.

Up the corridor. Still no noise. But a problem. The loose piece of plaster was gone and so was the key.

I searched up and down the corridor. Jesus Christ it felt risky hanging around like that. But like I said, I had to find out one way or the other.

Stupid. Didn't the door have a frame? First place you should always look. I tapped my hand along the top and sure enough, there in the dust, was the key. Not too bright after all, Christy.

I took it down and fitted it to the big steel padlock.

*Click.*

# 12

He was asleep, one hand nestled against his face and the blanket pulled up to his chin. The chain was coiled below his ankle like a watching viper. For a moment I thought about going away and letting him sleep, he looked so peaceful, but then I thought No.

'Haxforth,' I whispered. 'Haxforth.'

I reached out and touched his shoulder.

'Haxforth.'

His eyes flicked open. There was no tiredness in them, they were big and round and coloured like ivory and they seemed to dance out of sleep instantly like mine never did. 'I was dreaming,' he said quietly.

'What about?'

'Kings. Monsters. A face I saw once.'

'OK,' I said.

He threw the blanket aside and sat up and then stood.

Huddled in the thin dawn light wearing that sports gear he looked like the lonely victim of an earthquake, like something you'd see on the TV news.

Things change fast, these things that decide your Long Term Future. I'd gone through the door desperate to see him and for a moment or two, standing there in that tumbledown place with its high smashed windows and its squashed beer cans and the Pacific Blue still neglected in the shadows, I'd been ecstatic seeing that he – it – was all real. I wouldn't have to go calling for the loony wagon any time soon. It was like a mountainside of black grinding pressure had slipped off my back.

All I had to do was walk away and get on with my life.

Only here's the thing. Now I was getting pulled into *his* situation. A prisoner with a chain around his ankle, dressed in rags practically. A reason why he had to be there. And even if he didn't seem too bothered himself, unless someone did something soon it was possible – probable – he'd end up dead. His body might stay hidden *forever* in that old wreck of a building. Who would ever know?

Food. Why hadn't I brought any? Haxforth was malnourished, anyone could see that. Probably it was affecting his thinking and that was why he didn't seem to care too much about himself.

'I should have brought you something to eat,' I said stupidly. 'I didn't think.'

'Pity. I've been through leaner times, but not many.'

'I've got this though.'

I showed him the hacksaw and he reached out an old white hand, felt the blade with his thumb like I'd done outside.

He shrugged. *Try if you want to*, he seemed to be saying.

Silence – only a bird flittering in a far corner of the storeroom. Sheltering against the winter, most likely. At least it could come and go whenever it wanted, through those broken windows.

'Don't you ever leave this room?'

'Sometimes. They've taken me out to the countryside once or twice.'

'The countryside? Look, just tell me what it is they're after.' Knowing it was true, everything I'd seen the time before, made me want to know *why*. Something weird was going on in that place, something under the surface, more than gangs or money or whatever. But Haxforth didn't answer, only hunched against the cold and stared at me with those eyes that seemed to say everything and nothing, all at the same time.

I looked around, not knowing what to do next. Then I heard myself say, 'My mum, she thinks about monsters and stuff like that a lot. Only she doesn't dream about them, they talk to her when she's awake. Lots of things talk to her. They make her act crazy.'

I don't know why I did it, really. I'd never spoken about Mum like that to *anybody*. Maybe it was all those early-morning mail runs. Important stuff spills out easier when you're tired and worn right down. Or maybe it was the isolation of that place. It felt like you could tell a secret there and it'd stay vacuum-sealed forever, never leak into the wider world.

'Does she?' said Haxforth. 'Does she?'

'When it gets bad we have to hide all the knives.'

'Sometimes,' he said slowly, 'people hear messages from other places. Voices. They might not want anything to do with them, but that doesn't stop the messages coming. I have some experience with things of this—'

'It scares me,' I said, feeling my throat tighten suddenly. 'I want it to stop, I want to find a way of making it stop . . .'

I pressed the palm of my hand hard against the hacksaw blade. Toughen up, stop snivelling. One of Dad's sayings. I hadn't come back here to be a bleeding heart, to show this stranger everything that was hurting me.

'Come on,' I said roughly. 'I'm getting you out of here.'

We stretched the chain out, winding it round one of the pallets. My idea was to keep it tight, pinned to the splintery wood, to cut between the slats. Haxforth pointed at a link in the chain close to his ankle, the one he thought was the weakest, then he yanked the chain taut and stood on it with his feet apart.

'If you hear anything, anyone coming or anything, tap me on the shoulder straightaway.'

He nodded. I put the hacksaw to the chain and drew back the blade. My ears were ringing with the silence, ringing with trying to hear danger as far away as possible.

I started to saw. And oh god oh Jesus it was loud. I mean *really* loud. The silence of the morning and the silence of the abandoned factory and then that rasping and ripping tearing it all apart. Anyone out on the road would hear it. Anyone on the other side of *town* probably.

I sawed like mad for two minutes thinking, Get through it fast, get through it fast, then I stopped and got my breath back and looked up at Haxforth and looked down at the chain.

There was the tiniest silver groove in the link I'd been working on.

'Move it across,' I panted. 'It's wobbling too much between the slats. Get it on the wood.'

Haxforth made the adjustment but in the new position I

couldn't get the angle I needed. The blade was coming in too low, brushing the metal instead of cutting it. A splinter from the pallet jabbed sharp against my knuckles.

'Move it back,' I said. 'Stand on it there. I'm going to cut right on the edge.'

That was better. I went at it again, this time for longer, five minutes, six minutes, shredding the morning silence. My arm was going to drop off, I saw blood on the knuckles – but on I went, sawing, sawing, till my muscles screamed and I was drowning in a sea of gnashing sweating metal.

I pulled away, breathing hard.

I was maybe a tenth of the way through one side of the link.

Haxforth sat down and examined the chain. He picked up the hacksaw and felt the blade again and then laid it on the floor.

'You're acting like a peasant,' he said, in a resigned sort of way. 'A peasant is stupid. He does the same bad job with the same bad tools year after year and he wonders why life never gets any better.'

'What do you mean?'

'I mean you could sit there all day with that thing and not get through. We need a better tool. A sharper saw.'

'There's no time for that! What about—'

'Christy and his friends? Boys who think they're men. No imaginations. Not really so dangerous.'

'But your ankle! The blood supply's practically cut off!' My head was hot and spinny and I suppose I felt a bit desperate then, trying and failing like that.

'It looks worse than it is,' Haxforth said. 'And if you got through the chain – did you have a plan after that? Or were you going to release me like a caged bird?'

I didn't answer. I hadn't thought that far ahead – didn't think I'd need to.

'If you'd used your head you wouldn't even be here,' he said quietly. 'You'd have taken one look at me and left me to rot.'

'I needed my bike. And then I sort of . . . decided to come back . . .' I knew that was the moment to snatch at the question still hanging there in the air. 'That thing you said just now, about hearing voices, you talked about it like you'd seen it before . . .'

'I have. I've a brother, he heard things like that once, a long time ago.'

That got me super-interested, if I wasn't already.

'Heard them? You mean he doesn't any more?'

Haxforth shook his head. 'It has been a *very* long time, however.'

'I keep asking,' I said, 'but nobody'll tell me anything about it. What does it mean? What does it mean when somebody hears voices inside their head?'

'It means trouble.' Haxforth picked up the blanket, draped it over his shoulders. 'Homelessness – think of it like that. The mind is a palace and the person you know is the king who lives there, controlling everything. Well, something's come along and kicked out the king. That person you know and love – all of a sudden they've nowhere to go. They're outside time. And the servants, the thieves and creeps who've been at the bottom, the ones filled with rage and jealousy, they've taken over and they're shouting louder than anyone else, and they won't stop shouting and they can't agree on anything except that they don't want to give back the palace. That's what it means.'

I didn't say anything. I picked up the saw and looked at the blade. It wasn't sharp, never had been. I'd just been kidding myself, pumped up with stupid courage.

'Can you do anything to get rid of them?' It sounded pathetic and pleading, I realised that, but I needed to know. 'Can anyone? The voices, I mean?'

'What a question.' His two bleached-out eyes stared at me. 'I did something once, to help. Before I became one of the thieves.'

'Where exactly have you come from, Haxforth?'

'The houses of the rich. Mostly.'

A shadow flitted at the high smashed windows – the winter-sheltering bird heading out to greet the morning. Outside, the sky was turning from dark to light grey. Low cloud, day beginning, cars on the road.

Cars on the road.

All at once the questions and ideas whirling round my head were sinking faster than torpedoed ships. One vehicle in particular had separated itself off from the general hum. Closer it came, closer and closer.

The engine paused a moment, then whined as it backed up right outside.

# 13

Immobilised. That's how I felt, like the pictures you see on TV of the police shooting someone with a taser where the victim can't move or even hardly breathe. I'd only seen Christy in person for a few minutes but somehow the idea of him had grown inside – the idea of what he was capable of. And I was afraid, physically afraid, which wasn't a feeling I experienced too often and took a moment or two to process.

'Wait. Take this.' Still wrapped in the blanket, Haxforth went to the limit of the chain and reached his little finger into a crack in the concrete floor. 'Something I've managed to keep hidden from them.'

He thrust something into my hand but there was no time to see what, it was a small slender thing and already it was in my pocket.

'I find gold usually makes people come back.'

'I'm coming back anyway.'

'Yes,' he said. 'I know you are.'

Outside, the engine switched off.

'Don't forget the hacksaw,' he hissed. 'And the padlock.'

'What? Oh no!' I'd dropped the key to the padlock, the padlock that secured the door to his room, into another of my pockets and now it was buried deep where I couldn't find it.

Car doors slammed.

'Quickly,' said Haxforth. I felt him pushing me away and as he did so the blocked-up sludge in my veins whooshed back once more into real flowing blood and I ran, fumbling, searching for the key. There it was, hiding in the seam under my torch. I yanked it out hot already in my hand and raced into the corridor, closing the door, fiddling with the padlock, hands shaking and the thing not closing, not going in properly. I tipped up on my toes and put the key back on the dusty top of the door frame then tried the lock again. Still no go. I heard a clunking noise, a heavy external door being opened somewhere. They were inside already. Voices approaching, getting nearer. Christy's voice – the salt and scabs in the throat, no mistaking it. One last go at the lock to Haxforth's room and I'd have to run, whatever happened.

*Click*. The lock closed and I was out of there.

But where? Not up to the roof – that was the direction they were coming from, past the stairs, cutting me off. Nowhere else to go but the next door along. The old works canteen, the lines of ancient orange furniture. And then as I darted into the darkest corner of that room I saw and remembered the random angry dents in the wall that someone had sledgehammered months or years before. Dim ragged lights showed where a couple had broken right through the breeze block to next door. They were no bigger than cricket balls but I reckoned if

I got into the right position I might be able to see Haxforth sitting on his bed of pallets.

Down on all fours, stretching and angling my neck. Face well away from the hole.

Here they come.

'This time we'll nail the bastard, you see if we don't.'

'Take it easy, Christy. He's simple, don't you get it? We don't want a *body* on our hands. The cops'll be all over this place with their little forensics teams and their DNA, then they'll be round yours for a swab. They've got mine already. That what you want, is it?'

'Stay focused, Deano. You want to be nicking silly little stuff the rest of your life?'

'No, no, but go easy, that's all I'm saying.'

They were at Haxforth's door, opening the padlock. They were inside the storeroom with all the stolen stuff, with Haxforth and his chain and the primitive bed. The jailors surrounding the jailed.

For a moment nobody spoke. Then, 'I'm sick of you, you bloody retard,' Christy said, all loud and aggressive. 'I don't know why we're bothering. You're a ghost.'

Haxforth didn't answer. He was huddled down on the pallets, the blanket pulled up over his head and close round his throat like sometimes you see little kids do.

'I get the feeling that if one day you disappeared, no-one would care. No-one would even notice.'

'You're right,' Haxforth agreed.

'You can walk out of here today,' Deano said. 'This morning. Carry on to – wherever it was you were going. Wouldn't that be nice? Only tell us where the *rest of it* is.' You knew by his voice how uncertain he was about the whole thing, how he was looking for a way out just as much as Haxforth was.

'I don't know,' Haxforth said. 'Everything's changed, since I was here last. Even the hills look different.'

'Even the hills? What you going on about?'

'Tell us about the bracelet again,' Christy demanded. 'Tell us how it's linked with the other stuff, all the stuff you told us about when we found you on that path.'

'I was hungry then. I hadn't eaten in two days. I was delirious, I don't remember what I said.'

'You *said* you found it in a cave, that you knew where there was loads more stuff like it.'

'I did, but that's all there was. There's nothing else there now.'

'Damn right there isn't. Sixty miles we drove, to find that out. It wasn't even a proper cave!'

'We fed you, didn't we?' said Deano. 'We saved your life. So tell us where the rest of it is.'

'I don't know. I must have been confused. There isn't any more . . .'

'Your story keeps changing, doesn't it?' Christy said. 'Because that's not what you told us to begin with. Not at all. We think you need to *do better*. We think it's time for *specifics*.'

I dipped my head, trying to get a better view.

Be very very careful.

'Chocolate?' A head hovered close to the pallet bed and for a moment I saw Christy's face, a pugged-up nose and two eyes round with anger.

'Yes, please,' Haxforth said.

'Come and get it then.' The head bobbed away.

Haxforth stood, held out his hand. The grey Admiral hoodie

hung like a skirt about his knees. Christy punched him once, hard, in the stomach and as he flew back across the wooden pallets Haxforth looked straight at me, straight through the cricket-ball-sized hole at me with those colourless depthless eyes. A coin-sized dollop of blood was seeping already from between his pinched-together lips.

'You don't wander around with a bracelet like that, made of solid gold, and forget everything about it,' bellowed Christy. 'What is it – Roman? Something *ancient* anyway. It's worth a fortune, even I can see that!'

Haxforth mumbled something I couldn't hear. He was doubling up, pulling the greasy blankets and clothes around him as tight as he could.

Christy made a sort of gurgling noise in his throat and then he let rip.

'Just bloody –'

Kick.

'Tell us –'

Kick.

'Where!'

Kick.

'Bloody ghost!'

I shrank away from the hole. I wanted to scream out, You've already locked him up and starved him you cowards. What more do you want? But I didn't. I ran. Fear made me fast and soundless. Down the corridor, through the field of rusting machines, up the stairs thick with pigeon droppings. At the door to the roof I could still hear Haxforth grunting and crying out in pain.

Mum bent up in the corner. Me panicked I was going schizo like her. Haxforth being kicked and beaten. It was all getting mixed up in my head, all the nightmare things crashing in together.

Me on the roof, tears dropping off my chin.

I didn't bother with school.

# 14

It was winter-dark outside, beginning to rain, and the cup of tea I'd made a minute ago was cold already in my hands. I sat at the kitchen table. The clock on the microwave said 09.35. I had an idea what they'd be doing in class – trying to make us speak gobfuls of useless French again – but I didn't care enough to worry about it.

For the twentieth or maybe thirtieth time I looked at the thing Haxforth had given me. It was a clasp, a coiled hinge like a safety pin at one end and an arrowhead catch at the other. It lay there in my hand, small and heavy and yellow with deep lines down its length like waves on the sea. How nice it would be to sit staring at it all day, I thought. How nice to just do that and nothing else.

There was a knock on the door. Automatically I stood up to answer and it wasn't until I saw the big burly figure in the frosted glass that I thought maybe I should be upstairs hiding instead. But by then it was too late. The big burly figure was tapping on the glass, asking where Dad was.

I opened the door.

'All right, Aidan,' said the man. He was wearing shorts even though it was December and he had big black tattoos down both legs. Royal Mail boots, Royal Mail coat. The same guy I'd overheard once calling me a *skinny streak of piss*.

'All right, Hawkie,' I said.

'Where's your dad then?'

'At work.'

'He's not. Least, he's not where he should be.'

I shrugged.

'Can you tell him when you see him that I came round?'

'Yeah, OK.'

'He hasn't been answering his phone, that's all.'

'I'll tell him.'

He looked at me closely. 'Shouldn't you be at school?'

'Dentist's appointment,' I lied.

Hawkie turned to go, turned to walk out of the passageway and back into the rain. 'What time's he getting home from work these days?'

'Not really sure,' I said.

'All right, all right. Just remember. I need to talk to him.'

'I won't forget.'

I went out into the street and watched Hawkie till he disappeared round the corner. The sky was like a lump of dough with all its living yeast particles dead and extinct but the rain felt good for once, soft and clean on my skin and not too cold. I went back through the gate and passageway, into the garden and over to the shed.

The shed. I swear Dad didn't even go inside it any more.

Just glanced around to make sure the neighbours weren't watching before he chucked the stuff in and went back to the house. Back to his three places, the kitchen table, the sofa, the bed. Back to chips and curry sauce. Back to sitting and staring.

Three weeks he'd been doing it, ever since the start of Mum's breakdown when the witches and warlocks and world leaders started meaning more to her than we did. At first I didn't think it mattered. I tried to kid myself this was part of his routine, something I'd never noticed before. Then when I couldn't pretend any longer I told myself that even if it was wrong it didn't really matter. It wasn't important, not like if he'd murdered someone and buried the body or robbed a bank or cheated some old biddy out of her life savings.

Stupid me.

Because at school, researching a project online, I saw this news story by accident:

***Postman Jailed after Filling Flat with Stolen Mail***

*Matthew Greenwood, 26, of Erdington, Birmingham, was today jailed for 14 months after admitting the theft of more than 20,000 items of mail. Greenwood, a Royal Mail employee since leaving school at 16, had hidden so much post in his flat that he was unable to enter his own bedroom, bathroom or kitchen.*

*The massive theft, which had been carried out over a year-long period, only came to light when Greenwood's bath sprung a leak. James Garrard, a plumber who had been called in by a couple who lived downstairs from Greenwood, said: 'When I arrived at the property, water was pouring through the ceiling. I knew right away it was mains, so after knocking on Greenwood's door and getting no reply I called the letting agency. As it was an emergency, they gave me permission to break in. The mail almost fell on top of me when the door gave way. The first thing I did was call the police.'*

*Greenwood admitted interfering with mail, criminal damage and arson, as he had earlier tried to destroy the evidence.*

*Judge Charles Duncan said: 'You have caused immense distress to thousands of people as you wilfully stole from them and neglected your duties. Among the items you attempted to destroy were irreplaceable family photographs and a present for a sick child. In such cases the public expects a custodial sentence, and today that is what I am giving you.'*

*Outside court a spokesman for Royal Mail said: 'The vast majority of our postmen and women are honest, hard-working people who will always go that extra mile to deliver the mail safely and speedily. Thankfully cases like this are extremely rare. There can be no excuse for Greenwood's behaviour, and we will always prosecute anybody who abuses their position of trust in our organisation.'*

I read it twice, three times, to make sure I'd understood it right. I hit the print button. And then all I remember is sitting there in the computer suite going hot and cold with panic.

That's Dad, I thought. That's what my dad's doing. Only he hasn't been caught yet. Something happened to him when Mum went nuts and now he can't handle being a postman any more and he's taking his mail home from work and hiding it in our garden shed.

That man in the news story got fourteen months in prison for doing the same thing.

And then I thought, If Mum's in hospital and Dad's in jail, what's going to happen to me?

I'll be taken away, that's what. Put into some care home, miles from anywhere, miles from Mum, some place like a prison itself where you're locked down all the time and where the staff come into your room at night with sweets even though you know it's not the sweets they're really interested in.

So I was doing Dad's job. Or at least I was trying to, in the dark and in secret, until he pulled out of this thing that was making him stay in bed or stop in front of the TV for days on end.

I knew the route pretty well. How for example Lowther Road looped back on itself so that if you were ready with the post for Ferndale Terrace you could save time. How there was a little alley on Cant's Lane where you could get through to the Bowcliffe flats without going all the way around. How on Annandale Avenue the numbers went up in order rather than odds one side and evens the other. How 49 Old School Place had tight black bristles inside the letterbox which ripped the mail if you weren't careful. Complaints were the last thing Dad needed. The dog at 122 Cheswood Road who dozed by the door and started barking if you were too loud, and the man on Ingram Way who left for work each morning at exactly the same time in his big silver BMW, and how the water gushed across the road on Kingfisher Drive every time it rained, turning the junction into a swimming pool.

I knew it all. Just like Dad.

Every night after he went to sleep I'd take out the mail and sort it in my room. Loads of it was junk, selling pizzas or broadband or charity, and all that stuff I slung back inside the shed, as far from the door as possible. At first I tried putting it in carrier bags and dumping it but I soon stopped that, there was too much. Everything else I arranged by street and house number and stuffed into the Big Bag, an old zip-up cricket thing of Dad's with enough space for bat and pads and helmet. Once it was full it was about all I could do to carry it and get on the bike at the same time. My heavy, heavy homework. I came off a couple of times at first but it soon got lighter once you'd done a few streets. A cricket bag in December – it made me laugh. But nobody saw me, nobody made the connection. I didn't want them to either. It'd mean awkward questions.

Only, however hard I tried, however early I got up, the mail never stopped. It never went down. It was filling up the shed. I thought about it all the time, I dreamed about it crashing down on me, choking me, suffocating me. Collapsing paper houses, the Queen's head flickering in front of my face, eyes fierce, full of punishment. Feet changing shape as I tried to run away.

And now Christmas was coming – coming fast. Every day the post was getting heavier, a stream turning into a torrent turning into a river. A river inside a shed.

The shed. I went over to it, pulling back the black bolt that didn't even lock. Piles of mail, snowdrifts almost, new deposits left since I last opened the door so that straightaway a fresh panic threatened because how much longer could I *really* stay on top of this? I kicked my way inside though, taking care to stop the letters and packets and parcels from falling through the open doorway, doing my best to focus instead on the yellow clasp with the arrowhead catch still lying back on the kitchen table.

Prison. Trying to keep Dad out when I knew someone who was already in one.

I looked along the high tool shelves thick with grey granular dirt. There was nothing else there that'd cut chain, but then I'd known that anyhow. It didn't matter, I had a different plan now. A new plan.

The mail. Somewhere in that mountain of post there'd be cash, folded fives and tens and twenties. They were meant for someone else, but they had my name on them now. I'd resisted before but this was an emergency. You didn't have to be much of a guesser to know which items to try: the ones that looked like birthday cards, in their colourful square-shaped envelopes. Or anything in fact with weak glue, anything you could open easily and then reseal and smooth down and no-one ever knows. If it meant a few items having to go undelivered – well, that was just a risk I'd have to take. The alternative was leaving Haxforth to starve, or be beaten to death by Christy and his little tribe of psychopaths.

Find the money, take the money, buy a hacksaw, brand new. Then back to the Brace Brothers factory, cut the chain, get Haxforth over to that place on Northcote Road.

They ran a homeless hostel of some sort there, I felt pretty certain.

# 15

Thank you (and sorry):

Mrs M. Montague of 39 Wren's Nest Close – £5

Philip Lewry of Harefield Road – £10

Ms Annie Fraser-Howe of Flat 6, Langney Place, Totland Terrace – £50

Fifty pounds.

I couldn't believe it when *that* dropped out from between the thin handwritten sheets inside the envelope. A fifty-pound note. I'd never held one or even seen one before. Pink and red and silver-stripped, two men with their high collars and steam-age inventions and that weird thing they all have written on them, I PROMISE TO PAY THE BEARER ON DEMAND . . .

I looked at it, examined it. The detail was incredible, all the little traps they'd put in to stop forgers. I realised I was holding my breath, trying to decide what to do.

Five pounds from Mrs Montague and ten from Philip Lewry. Surely fifteen pounds would buy a new hacksaw? Why was I going on, opening more letters, prying into the lives of people like Annie Fraser-Howe?

Because I could. Because I was getting greedy. I knew I couldn't rely on Dad for dinner money or anything else. My phone'd already been cut off because he hadn't paid the contract. See, the one thing about money and needing it but not being able to get it any normal way is that it stops you acting nice. It makes doing things like stealing seem OK. And if the chance comes along for a bit extra, you take it, because that extra might mean SAFETY.

Every thief for himself – isn't that what Haxforth said?

All the same, I stared at that big pink note for a long time.

OK.

Stop.

Breathe.

Count to twenty.

I folded it up and stuck it in my back pocket. This is the first time, I told myself. Make sure it's the last. It wasn't like I could really do it again anyway, in case it came back to bite Dad some day.

I looked down at the letters scattered about my bedroom, the latest load from the shed. I'd smuggled them in under my coat, opened maybe sixty or seventy to get to those three banknotes, slicing carefully under the envelope-flaps using one of the sharp knives we'd hidden from Mum. All of them I could seal back up and deliver tomorrow. All except those three. I gathered them up, those three, hid them behind my fake-wood chest of drawers, then I shoved the rest of the mail under the bed and pulled the quilt down to the floor just-got-up-style.

Outside in the rain I unlocked the racing bike. Dad still hadn't noticed that the Pacific Blue had gone. Where was he anyway? Visiting Mum at Tredegar House? Delivering post like Royal Mail paid him to?

Fat chance.

I cycled over to the shopping park, the three banknotes tucked safe into my jeans alongside the clasp. Part of me was already spending that money, and not in B&Q.

'Where are your hacksaws?' I asked a young tattooed guy in an orange apron. 'I need the sharpest one you've got.'

'They're all sharp.' He dug something out, a bit of dirt, from beneath a fingernail. 'What is it you want to cut?'

'Bit of chain,' I said.

'How thick?'

'About so.' I showed him with my thumb and forefinger.

'Take you ages with a hacksaw. I'd use a bolt cutter instead.'

'Can you show me where they are?'

'This way.'

We stopped in front of a wall of tools and he took down something like a pair of garden shears with a snubby nose and two long handles. 'Careful,' he said. 'It's heavy. You put your chain in there and push. Cut anything, that will.'

I weighed the bolt cutters in my arms. I could see right away they'd do the job. They'd fit into the Big Bag OK, too.

'How much are these?'

'Don't know. Eighteen quid or something. Whatever it says on the tag. Pay at the front of the shop.'

The woman at the till looked at me funny when I handed over the fifty but I stared her out and she gave me the change fine.

# 16

The rain'd stopped by the time I got home. I'd spent quite a while inside a cafe, staring out at the town's lights and all their puddled reflections, cups of tea and a Full English courtesy of Annie Fraser-Howe and the others I'd pinched from. Now it was afternoon, past three. Soon the plan in my head, the invisible lines leading to Haxforth's release, would be real and achieved. Whatever else happened after that, I could go back to concentrating on the Christmas rush.

I got the bike secured and the bolt cutters hidden inside the Big Bag then went to put my key in the door, thinking and assuming the house to be empty. There was someone moving around in the kitchen though. A moment later Dad opened the lock from the other side.

'Leave your coat on,' he said. 'We're going straight out.'

'Out? Where?'

'I'm taking you over to Tredegar House for an hour or so.'

'But I thought you said . . .'

'Forget what I said and take these.'

We sat silent in the car, caught in a line of traffic. The blue tin of chocolates that he'd handed me rested cold on my knees. Dad, pale and serious, watched the road. I watched the red brake lights going off and on in front of us. The people in the streets were wrapped in their winter gear, everyone carrying bags of Christmas shopping.

'They want to make things as normal as possible for her,' Dad said at last. 'Surround her with things she knows. That's why they think it'd be good for her to see you.'

I didn't say anything. He'd never taken me before, even though I'd asked him to loads of times. Now the reality of actually going made me feel sort of numb.

'There's a chance she might not recognise you,' said Dad. 'When I went in yesterday it took a couple of minutes before she remembered who I was. And she's put on some weight. A lot of it's down to the medication they're giving her.'

'You told me you didn't go in yesterday! Day before yesterday, you said!'

'Did I?'

'Yes!'

'Well, it doesn't matter now.' Dad took his eyes off the car in front and looked across at me, not making proper eye contact though. 'I'm doing my best.'

Your best isn't good enough, I wanted to shout but didn't.

'There's a pattern,' he said. 'You're not old enough to know it but there's a pattern. We'll get through this just like we did last time.'

Last time. I don't remember too much about that. It was three years ago, maybe more. One minute Mum was there and then suddenly she wasn't and no-one would tell me where she'd gone. When she came back it was like something was missing, but I could never work out if it was just me or whether she'd always been like that and I'd been too young to notice.

'Is she still hearing voices?' I asked.

'What do you know about that?'

'I heard the doctor talking about it, when the ambulance came.'

'You should have been asleep,' Dad said sadly. 'It was the middle of the night, then. A boy your age needs all the shuteye he can get.'

I went back to gazing at the red brake lights. Are you having a laugh, I thought – or what? Don't you *know* I'm getting up in the small hours and going out in the fog and the freezing rain every morning to do *your* job?

No. He didn't know. He really didn't.

The car park at Tredegar House was gravelled so you couldn't approach it silently. Every footstep felt like a tiny sinking or sucking that you needed to make an extra effort to escape from. The lobby was bright, hygienic, empty. Even the little office behind the enquiries desk stood quiet, its computer screen dissolving into endless multicoloured patterns.

We took the lift to the fourth floor and walked along a yellow-painted corridor until we reached a wooden door with a big metal handle and an oblong of reinforced glass. Dad pressed the buzzer and said, 'Visitor for Mary Hale,' and after a couple of minutes a nurse wearing a plastic apron opened the door and beckoned us in. Then there was a second door like an airlock where the nurse swiped a card through an entry point and inched inside. She had to do that because somebody was blocking the door, trying to slip out even though she was right there.

'Mr Allum,' the nurse said, like she was talking to a child, 'please move out of the way. Can't you see there's people trying to come in?'

An old man with thin white hair and a red scalp stared at us. I think the T-shirt he wore said Harley-Davidson but it was difficult to tell because he had most of it stuffed into his wet chewing mouth. The whole front of the T-shirt was soaked. As the nurse manoeuvred him away a string of loose saliva spattered on her plastic apron.

'Sorry about that,' she said, glancing up at a whiteboard where Mum's name was written along with lots of others. 'Down here, please.' She led us along another yellow-painted corridor, past leather sofas smelling of public toilets. Through an open door I could see people sitting in a circle, heads nodding but nobody talking. I looked backwards. Harley-Davidson man was following us, shuffling fast to keep up like he was one of the family. As soon as we got inside Mum's room, Dad slammed the door in his face.

'Mrs Hale,' the nurse said brightly, 'some visitors for you. Would you like me to stay?'

Mum made some kind of noise that the nurse took to be no. 'I'll be back shortly then. I think they've brought you some chocolates, you lucky thing.'

Alone with Mum, in Mum's room. A bed, a chair, a bedside cabinet. Nothing else. No curtains to draw back or close. Beige blinds and bars on the outside instead.

'Hello, love,' Dad said. 'How are you feeling today?'

Mum said nothing.

'She's right about those chocolates. Look, biggest tin I could find. Here –' he prised open the tin and rummaged around inside and I saw that his hands were shaking slightly – 'an orange one. Your favourite. And Aidan's come this time, to see you. Here, Aidan, give this to your mum.'

I took the chocolate and went over to the bed. I sat on the edge of the bed. I pressed the shiny crackling orange wrapper into Mum's hands.

Mum.

She looked like a fat folded-up snowman. Tiny tiny black eyes that never blinked, great thick cold arms, legs lost in the white bedsheets.

'Mum . . .' I couldn't say any more because something hard was caught in my throat.

'Come on, Aidan,' Dad said. 'Don't snivel. She doesn't need to see that from you right now.'

'Sorry,' I gulped.

We sat there in silence. One minute. Two minutes. Three. Dad went over to the oblong of glass in the door and looked through. Harley-Davidson man had gone.

'Back in a bit,' he said. 'I'm going to find one of the nurses to talk to. You OK, being in here on your own?'

I nodded Yes.

He closed the door softly behind him and I sat there alone, looking at Mum.

It's weird. I'd imagined that situation a lot – what I'd say to her if nobody else was around. There were so many things. There was even a little part of me that thought by saying all those things, by sharing them, they'd somehow have the power to make her better. But now that moment was here, nothing would come out. I stared at her, trying to find a way to start, and then I realised *she* was trying to speak to *me*.

'Mum?'

I leaned in closer.

'Mum?'

Something was coming out from between her lips, that was certain. Some sort of whispering. But hard as I tried I couldn't find any sense in it. It was more like a song you hear being hummed in the distance, all the sounds running together. And it only lasted a moment or two. Then the silence returned.

'Mum, it's me, it's Aidan . . .'

She moved her head, gazed out of the window. One of her legs started shaking under the blankets and bedclothes. She rolled over onto her side, stayed there where I couldn't see her face.

Quietness grew around us. It expanded and expanded. The shaking in the leg slowed and then stopped. It was like we were two objects in outer space, two objects whose orbits'd never synchronise again.

The door opened. Dad returning. 'Has she said anything?' he asked, coming over to the bed.

'I – I don't—'

'She's only just had her medication. It can knock them right out, that's what they say. But the nurses think she's improving, overall.'

'Improving?' I managed to get the word out, just.

Dad shrugged. 'Things going in the right direction.'

I looked at him, wanting to know more, but he didn't say anything else. Perhaps he didn't have anything else *to* say. I didn't know if he was kidding himself, or trying to protect me, or what he was doing. All I knew was how could there be any improvement, any talk of improvement, if Mum couldn't even recognise or talk to us?

'She's probably exhausted. We should let her rest. Maybe this wasn't the best time to come after all.'

I got up, and it was about the hardest getting-up-from-a-bed that I'd ever done. I thought of the wedding-day picture, the one on the mantelpiece at home. This wasn't the same person. It couldn't be. Slim and blonde and beautiful, Dad not believing his luck. Both of them still teenagers. But it was. The confusion in Mum's eyes on that long-ago day led straight to this hospital room. Straight to the bars on the window and the medication that was making her obese.

The doctors say she's got schizophrenia.

Haxforth says people like this are hearing messages from other places.

I didn't know who or what to believe just then. Sometimes, maybe all the time when you come right down to it, no amount of book-reading or cleverness helps. You can only ever know how you feel. Right then, it was like somebody was booting me in the stomach every hour of every day.

# 17

8.38, the lopsided clock in Miss Tuckett's classroom window said. I sat on the low wall by the gates and watched the schoolyard filling up. There, coming along the path, was Daniel Cushway. He'd have to walk right past where I was sitting if he wanted to get inside. I saw him glance at me and then away. How stupid all of that had been – having to stamp and shout around him just so I could eat. Like some conspiracy to keep me being a tiny kid forever. Well, I didn't need his money any more, not with so much left over from those three envelopes I'd sliced open in secret.

I turned Haxforth's clasp over in my pocket. That was where it lived now, safe and secure. I thought of the beating he'd taken, the kick kick kick. Haxforth, who I'd let down, who I should've got out of that terrible place by now. The truth was, after seeing Mum in Tredegar House it was about all I could do to close the door of my bedroom and climb under the quilt until it was time to get up and start the early-morning mail round. And even then I'd done *almost nothing* because of sleeping somehow through the alarm I kept under my pillow. So I knew I'd have to go at it doubly hard from now on, go at it relentless like a machine if all that stuff inside the shed wasn't to get completely out of control.

The nearer he got, the faster Daniel Cushway was walking. His head had gone down, avoiding eye contact. I didn't say anything as he went past. The pus-filled spot on the side of his nose looked worse today, like it was going to splat out any second. I thought of Christy and his pals, of the sort of people they were and what made them think they could treat Haxforth, or anyone, like that. And I thought too, at the same time, about all those things I'd been doing to Daniel Cushway.

I slipped off the wall and started walking after him.

'Daniel,' I called.

He stopped dead. Turned. I knew he was afraid. 'I haven't got any money for you,' he said. 'I can't give you any more.'

'It isn't that,' I said. 'I wanted to show you something.'

'What?' he said warily, knowing it might mean a fist in the face.

'Come here. Look.'

I gave him the clasp. He examined it, poked it about on the palm of his hand. I could see right away he was interested.

'What do you think? You know about history, don't you?'

I knew that because his house was one of my regular stops with the Big Bag, so I saw the type of post he got – things from the British Museum, magazines with names like *History Today*. Stuff like that, all addressed to D. CUSHWAY.

'My dad knows more about it than I do,' he said. 'Where did you get this?'

'Found it,' I said.

He poked it about a bit more. 'It's really old. But then it also sort of looks like it might have been made last week.' He looked at me closely, a look he'd never given me before. 'Where'd you find it?'

For the first time in his life Daniel Cushway wanted to talk to me rather than run away.

'I'm not going to tell you, yet. I might do later, if you promise not to tell anyone else.'

'I promise,' he said straightaway.

'And if you help me find out a bit more about it. Exactly how old it is.'

'You want *me*,' he said, 'to help *you*?' His eyes were blinking fast and I knew he wanted to say, What's in it for me? only he couldn't bring himself to.

'You can forget about bringing that money in every day,' I said. 'If you do.'

'Really?'

'Yeah.'

'OK,' said Daniel.

'Great. Give it here then.'

Daniel handed back the clasp. 'I'd take it to the museum,' he said. 'If I were you. Someone there might be able to tell us more about it.'

'Us?'

'You. Us. You asked me to help, didn't you?'

'Yeah. I did. All right. Where is it then exactly, this museum?'

'You mean you've never been there?'

'If I knew where it was I wouldn't be asking, would I?'

'It's down on Knowle Square. I could show you sometime.'

'Yeah?'

'Yeah.'

'When?'

Daniel looked around. The whistle had gone and the schoolyard was emptying. Miss Tuckett's clock said 8.49. Big black rainclouds were coming over and all the lights in the school were on, the windows misting up already.

'Now?' Daniel looked scared again but also a tiny bit excited.

'Brilliant,' I said, smiling.

# 18

The rain was coming down properly by the time we reached the centre of town. We would've taken the bus but Daniel said he didn't have enough money. Maybe that was true and maybe it wasn't. The museum steps were wide and empty and slick with wetness until you got to a sheltered bit at the top with stone columns where we stood and shook the water off our coats and Daniel smoothed down his hair.

'I've never done this before,' he told me. 'Bunking off school.'

'Nothing to it,' I said. 'Easy. 'Specially for you.'

'What do you mean?'

'You can make up any excuse when you get back and they'll buy it. Me – it'll be trouble again. Not that I care.' I put my fists up like an idiot and acted like a boxer sparring with the nearest column.

'I can't believe you've never been here before,' Daniel said.

'Well, I haven't, so shut up about it. Come on, let's go inside. Which way?'

'Through here.'

Inside the museum. Marble floors and high ceilings, the smell of cleaning fluid and dust. A few old people gliding around on legs that hardly worked any more, speaking in low murmurs or not speaking at all. A guard in a black-and-green uniform sat dozing at the end of a long corridor. The reception area was empty so we walked around for a bit through rooms full of porcelain, rooms full of pictures, rooms full of clocks and old musical instruments. Daniel had a long look at those. That was something he was famous for in our school, being good at music, playing the piano, stuff like that. Finally he caught sight of a man in brown jacket and trousers disappearing through a door.

'We'll ask him. He looks like he might know.'

The man was in a hurry, annoyed we were delaying him. He barely glanced at the clasp when I held it out. 'Looks like a bit of old tat to me,' he said. 'But then it's hardly my field. I'll get McKendrick to look at it, he's usually at a loose end this time of the day.'

We waited five, ten minutes by the door. We waited fifteen minutes. Daniel wandered away and looked into some more glass cases. What was I doing here? This wasn't my kind of place, never would be. I should be at home, smuggling more mail into my room from the shed, sorting it, making up for the time I'd lost last night.

Or I could be travelling the miles over to Tredegar House, trying perhaps to visit Mum on my own – see if she really had *improved*. I wondered if they'd let me in without an adult, without Dad. Something told me No. Would she even know who I was this time? This time, or next week, or next year?

Maybe she's gone for good.

Don't think it. Don't even think it.

'I've been told you have an Ancient Artefact for me to examine . . .' a sarcastic voice said close to my ear.

I jumped. They'd snuck up on me, whoever it was. 'What?' I said.

Daniel came running over. 'Are you Mr McKendrick?'

'I am,' replied the man, all whiskers and shirt collar and green checked jumper. I could see he was looking straight at Daniel's pus-filled spot but Daniel didn't seem to notice. 'And which of you boys has this Ancient Artefact?'

'I do,' I said. 'It belongs to me.'

'Of course it does. Well, let's see it then.' He let out a weird snuffly chortle. 'Don't worry, I promise not to keep it for the collection.'

I fumbled in my pocket, not liking the look of this man, not liking the way he talked or his disgusting green jumper and wondering whether I should even give the clasp to him or not but still watching myself hand it over anyhow.

Mr McKendrick held the clasp up and moved nearer to a window to get a better look. His eyes widened ever so slightly.

'Come with me,' he said briskly. 'Both of you.' He marched down a side corridor, opened a door and led us up a grey staircase. At the top another door opened onto an office. A secretary was doing something on a computer, steam floating up from a cup of tea beside her keyboard. Other doors led off to other places.

Mr McKendrick crossed to a desk drawer and rummaged around. 'Sandra,' he said, 'have you seen my magnifying glass? Some damn fool's moved it.'

The secretary stared at her computer screen and ignored him.

'Ah – here we are. Good. Now then . . .' He placed the clasp on the desk, on a large clean sheet of white blotting paper, and hung his head over the magnifying glass. Every now and then he pushed the arrowhead end or turned it over with a sharp-pointed pencil. When he was satisfied, he sat down in a chair and gazed at us very seriously.

'I want you to tell me where you got this from.'

Daniel looked at me expectantly.

'First I want you to tell me what it is,' I said. 'What it's worth.'

'Well, it's nothing much, I can tell you that. Anglo-Saxon, possibly.' His eyes flicked away, avoiding mine. 'A bit of old rubbish that kept someone's jewellery in place, I daresay.'

'It's solid gold,' I said.

'I realise that,' Mr McKendrick answered stiffly. The clasp was lying there on the white blotting paper, slightly nearer to him than to me.

'So it must be worth something,' I said, taking a step forward.

'Worth something? Oh yes, I should think so. But what was it buried with? That's the question.'

'I didn't find it in the ground.'

'No? Where then?'

'I can't say.'

'Can't? Or won't? How about you . . . ?'

'Daniel,' said Daniel, and I flashed him a look that said, What did you tell him your name for, you didn't have to do that you idiot.

'I saw it for the first time just now,' Daniel said.

'Which school do you both attend?'

From the corner of my eye I could see that the secretary had stopped staring at her screen and was now staring at us.

Neither of us said anything.

'Under the law, anyone finding something like this has to tell the authorities. And you came here, after all, to ask for help. Didn't you? To let the professionals take over . . .'

'I came here because I wanted to find out more about this –' I reached out for the clasp and as I did so Mr McKendrick's hand suddenly came down on mine, pinning it to the desk.

'You'll leave it here with us,' he said softly, 'of course. By law . . .'

'No I bloody won't,' I said, wrenching free but seeing at the same time how he'd snatched the clasp away with his other hand. So next thing I was wrestling him across the desk, lunging for the thieving fist of this disgusting green-jumpered man, hearing him let out a cry of surprise as I dug and levered in there with my thumb and saw the clasp go skittering away across the floor.

I saw Daniel scramble for it, pick it up – saw him look from me to Mr McKendrick and back again.

'Just bring that here,' Mr McKendrick told him, beckoning, 'and I'll forget about your friend's silliness.'

'You promised you wouldn't keep it,' Daniel said.

'That was before I knew what it was.'

Daniel shook his head. He dropped the clasp into his coat pocket. Then I shouted Run and past the open-mouthed secretary we flew, down the stairs, right in front of the black-and-green-uniformed guard who stood there like a lemon and through the reception area and out onto the wide grey steps which were bathed now in wintry sunshine. For a split second I stopped to look up at the skies, to look at the unexpected blue that had appeared in one big corner, a blue bluer even than the gold of the clasp was gold and then we were away.

Nobody came after us. Five streets on, nice and quiet, we stopped and put our hands to our knees and gasped for breath. Daniel's face was red and his chest heaving. He wasn't one of those who're too great at football, running, things like that.

'I didn't think you were going to do that!' I said.

'Neither did I. But he promised and then he tried to go back on it. People shouldn't ever break promises.'

'Suppose not.' He sounded like he really meant it and I wondered what'd happened to him to make him think like that because everyone knows people break promises all the time, that it's just something you have to get used to.

He brought the clasp out from his coat pocket. There in the winter sunshine it looked like a molten slash on his opened-up hand.

'Where did you get it?'

I knew I couldn't dodge the question this time. Handing the clasp over to Mr McKendrick would've been the easiest thing in the world for Daniel to do, but he hadn't, he'd refused. And then there was Christy and Deano and what I'd seen through the hole in the breeze block wall. Maybe it would be good if someone knew where I was going tonight and why.

His eyes were as wide as ten-pence pieces by the time I'd finished talking.

'Who? Who's doing all this to him?' he said.

'I don't know who they are exactly, but I know I don't ever want to meet them. They reckon he knows where there's more stuff like this clasp, lots more gold. It's weird, but I sort of think they might be right.'

'More of this?'

The clasp was still sitting in the palm of Daniel's hand. The coiled hinge and the arrowhead catch. If this once kept someone's jewellery in place, what must the jewellery itself have looked like?

'He talks about kings and monsters too. I mean, almost like he's seen them for real.'

Daniel stared at me hard. 'You're making all this up.'

'Come along if you don't believe me,' I said. 'I'm going at midnight.' I told him a place to meet – a concrete compound close to the roundabout, some place they used for electricity.

Daniel gave back the clasp and I stuffed it deep in my trousers pocket, the place where it lived now safe and secure. He knew about Haxforth but that didn't mean I'd told him anything about the mail I was delivering every night, hoping to keep Dad out of jail and me out of the care home. Every secret has its own depth, its own reasons for revealing or not revealing, and that wasn't a surface secret. No way. It wasn't heroic, like rescuing an old man from starvation. It was dark and shameful, one of those secrets that'll destroy you if you let even one millimetre of it out into the light.

'Maybe see you later then?' he said, a bit hesitant.

I shrugged. 'Yeah, maybe.'

He walked off in his direction, I walked off in mine.

# 19

Evening. Dad was sitting in front of the telly. It was dark outside but all the lights in the house were off apart from the one in the kitchen. A football pitch shone greenly across his face and body. I wondered what was going on inside that head of his – whether there was an official age when you stopped thinking, or at least stopped talking about what you were thinking about. See, what he really needed to do was open up some Lines of Communication, those things they're always going on about on daytime TV when the families scream at each other. But he couldn't. Whatever the reason, he just couldn't.

'The Arsenal,' he said, hearing me in the doorway. 'Going to be a tricky one. Need all three points. Sit down.'

I leaned in closer. The clock in the corner of the TV said twelve minutes.

'Might watch the second half,' I said.

'Suit yourself.' He had a can of lager in one hand and beside him on the brown sofa, in the place where Mum used to curl up, there sat a greasy mound of chip wrappers.

'Can I turn the heating on?' I asked. 'It's freezing upstairs.'

'Fine. Do you know how to?'

'Yeah, I'm not a kid. Mum showed me years ago.'

'Go on then.' He didn't blink when I mentioned Mum. Didn't say anything more about what'd happened at the hospital, or whether things really were getting better for her. It was like we'd never visited at all. He didn't ask me anything either, where I'd been, how school was, how I was, anything like that.

I poked the toe of my trainer into the place where the carpet was coming away. 'I forgot to tell you. Someone came looking for you yesterday. Your mate from work – Hawkie.'

That made him look up.

'Hawkie?'

'Yeah.'

Dad turned down the volume on the TV.

'What did he say?'

'Nothing. Just that he wanted to talk to you. Said you weren't answering your phone.'

'What did you say?'

'I didn't say anything. Told him I'd tell you, that's all. He asked what time you were getting home from your duties and then he went away.'

'I don't know why he's bothering,' Dad said, more to himself than to me. 'He's going full time with the union soon. Won't even be at our place any more. Wait a minute – what time was this? Why weren't you at school?'

'It was lunchtime,' I lied. 'I had to come home to get something.'

'Tell the truth, Aidan.'

'What about you telling the truth for once?' I shouted.

'What do you mean? What you talking about?' Dad jumped up, scrunching the chip papers, flinging them across the room. I thought maybe he wanted to put my head in with those wrappers and scrunch that up too.

'Nothing,' I said, backtracking fast.

'If there's something you want to say, Aidan, come right out and say it. Anything else is for cowards.'

*Cowards*. I couldn't believe what I was hearing. I was talking about Hawkie, I wanted to say, about you, your mail, all that stuff you're hiding in the shed. Don't you know you're going to get caught and when you do the judge won't give a stuff about Mum or what's happening inside her head and you'll go to prison and then I'll get shoved in a care home or something, I mean how stupid can they be at the mail centre, they must have worked it out by now, all that post gone missing, the knock could come any time, the cops could be parking their car and walking up to our house right now—

'Jesus Christ!' shouted Dad. 'Goal! You made me miss it!'

He turned back to the TV, the volume up, the little men running and grinning and pulling off their red-and-white shirts.

I fled upstairs.

# 20

There's one thing about being out on your own a lot at night-time and that's that you start getting some pretty crazy ideas. For example I kept thinking how I was in a sort of alliance with the moon. Every time I was out with the Big Bag I watched it change, go through what they call its phases. In a few nights' time it'd be at its fullest and already the strong white light meant I didn't always need my torch. Tonight though, when I needed to be soft-footed and invisible, it was locked tight behind cloud. So setting out, I knew the alliance was good.

It was after midnight. Power hummed smooth from the concrete compound behind me, the place where they made or stored electricity. I shifted the Big Bag on my shoulders. There wasn't any post in there though, only the bolt cutters sharp against my back. The rusting racer I'd left at home too. This wasn't the time to be getting tangled up in brakes and gears and chain.

Haxforth. Where's he going? The homeless shelter, yes, for a night or two, but after that? Next week, next year – where?

The houses of the rich. That's what he said. Does he go there to live? Or to steal and run?

That was assuming he could go *anywhere.* It was one hell of a kicking they'd dished out, Christy and his mate.

Time to move. I'd waited long enough, Daniel wasn't coming. In fact, thinking about it, I didn't know why I'd told him about Haxforth at all. His helping me in the museum like that must've made me go soft in the head. But it isn't any good, being soft, in this life. The only person you can rely on is yourself. No, Daniel would've been a liability. I was better off on my own.

I pulsed steam from my mouth and started walking, hugging the outside edge of the roundabout, trying to turn my body into a shadow. If you practise it long enough maybe you can do it for real. I knew anyway that as soon as I reached the factory the blood-drums would start up. They're good sometimes, when they're sounding it means you're running clear on instinct and don't have to think too much any more. Almost like you're a hunter, back in the time when there were no cities but only forests.

All these crazy night-time thoughts.

'Aidan,' hissed a voice.

'Jesus!' I spun round.

'Sorry. Didn't mean to surprise you.'

'You didn't,' I said quickly.

Daniel was dressed all in black. Black boots on his feet and a black scarf tucked into a high-zipped coat and up top a black woolly hat yanked close over his ears. He looked like he'd joined a special forces unit or something. Not that I laughed. I didn't really feel like it, what with one thing and another.

'Is it far?' he said. 'Where we have to go?'

'No, not far at all.'

'This better be real, because if it isn't . . .'

I unslung the Big Bag, showed him the bolt cutters. Seeing those, he knew I was serious. Knew I had Purpose and Intent. 'These'll free Haxforth in no time.'

'Haxforth?'

'That's his name – the old guy who gave me the clasp, who's chained up. Didn't I tell you?'

'You didn't tell me his name,' Daniel said.

We walked fast beyond the roundabout and on towards the industrial estate with its jumble of factories and warehouses. A few halogens hung suspended like slabs of supercharged ice around the newer units but the whiteness didn't penetrate anywhere near the derelict areas where we were headed. Daniel Cushway out at midnight, I was thinking that whole time. Well, well, well.

Down the weed-choked alley. At the end, the building that said Brace Brothers. The swishy-lettered sign, giving no clue about what they ever did inside.

No cars. No voices. Silence. Not even the wind blowing.

'In there,' I whispered.

'How do we get inside?'

'Follow me.' I glanced at Daniel. If he was scared, he wasn't letting it show. Why was he here? The clasp was interesting all right but it had to be more than that. I didn't feel I could ask him directly though. Maybe I'd never find out. You hardly ever find out anything properly about other people, not when you come right down to it.

We went around the building and in a flash of torchlight I showed him the weed-choked lower rungs of the fire-escape ladder.

'Up there,' I said.

'Right to the top?'

'Right to the top. You're not scared of heights, are you?'

'No.' He reached out and touched a rung, pulled back his hand. He wasn't wearing gloves and they were like knives, those metal rungs, frost-knives cutting flesh.

'Isn't there any other way in?'

'Not that I know of,' I said.

Daniel opened his mouth, to reply or make a suggestion perhaps. But what it was I'll never know because just then out of the endless midnight world we saw high-beam headlights angling in our direction. They weren't in any kind of a hurry but suddenly we were. Soon a familiar engine would be pushing its way through the overgrown avenues and alleyways of the industrial estate.

*Second time* of nearly being caught. Luck like that can't last forever.

'Get climbing!' I said. 'Quick!'

Up the ladder Daniel went, grasping the danger instantly because one thing about him at least he wasn't slow like that. I saw his feet slip-sliding on the white frosted metal, thought how if he fell I'd be right underneath but still taking hold of the ladder and following fast because after all what choice did I have. That climb must've only lasted half a minute but it felt longer, a lot longer. What with the bolt cutters banging against my back and Daniel's black boots clanging above my head and the frost-knives slicing my hands, and knowing what was inside and what down below, it was like everything was suddenly screaming DEATHTRAP.

Then I saw Daniel sprawled on the flat factory roof and I was next to him and for a minute we didn't do or say anything.

# 21

Christy and Deano and another of their scumbag helpers were bundling a figure out from the back of the Transit. The glow from the tail-lights showed the scene, the blanket covering the head, the figure surrounded and held on all sides – like a prisoner being led away to begin a life sentence.

'That's him,' I whispered. 'That's Haxforth.'

Daniel grabbed my arm to pull me back. I was leaning out over the wide square parapet that ran around the roof's edge, wanting to get a better view. He didn't need to worry though. People never think to look up.

I heard a lock and a door being opened. Whispered words, some scuffling. Then the angle cut off my view. It was too acute. They'd gone inside anyway.

'We need to call the police,' Daniel said in an undertone. 'This is really serious.'

'I know it's serious. That's why I've got these.' I nudged the Big Bag lying next to my spying position, indicated the bolt cutters inside.

'It's kidnapping and assault and –'

We crab-crawled away from the parapet, moved to the centre of the roof where it was safer to stand and talk. Daniel was taking something out of his pocket but I couldn't believe he was actually going to use it.

'Hold on a minute,' I said. 'We're going to go down there and cut him loose, just as soon as they've gone. That was the plan all along.'

'But what if they don't leave? What do we do then?'

I could see the numbers on the white electronic screen of his phone. He'd tapped them out already, the three nines. All he had to do was hit the green call button.

'Daniel,' I said, 'don't do that.'

With those numbers staring at me, all I could think was Police, Dad, Shed, Prison.

'Why not?'

'They won't do anything about it, they're useless.' My answer sounded flat and unconvincing and I knew it.

'They will. They'll be here really fast. They have targets for that sort of thing, responding to emergency calls.'

His thumb hovered over the dial button.

'Don't, I'm asking you, please.'

'I really think we should.'

He tapped the button and I snatched the phone out of his hand, slamming down on the screen before it could connect, knowing the cops always call back if a 999 call gets cut off. Then I took a step towards the parapet, held my arm back like I was about to hurl it over the edge.

Silence. In the darkness I could just make out Daniel's eyes fixed on me, blinking fast.

'It's right what they say at school.' His voice when he spoke trembled slightly. 'You're a psycho. Just like your mum.'

That got my head throbbing all right. Ordinarily, anyone saying that – well, the stone-hard fist-blocks would be up and going in hard. But I couldn't react that way now, couldn't chance it with Christy's van still down there and Haxforth inside too. So I did something I've hardly ever done before. I sucked it up. And part of that, part of the sucking-it-up, was thinking how even if Daniel *had* said it, even if he'd meant it in the nastiest way possible, it didn't stop the facts themselves being true. Mum *was* stuck in that terrible place along with all those other nutjobs. Hitting Daniel Cushway, or anyone else, wasn't going to change any of that, was it?

'If the bolt cutters don't work, you can call the police then,' I said. 'Anonymously though. No names. You have to promise me that.'

I was still holding the phone like a grenade ready to be lobbed.

'All right,' he said.

'Here.' I gave the phone back. Promises seemed to mean more to Daniel than they did to other people so I thought that was an OK thing for me to say, better than fighting anyway. I stared out at the town twinkling below us, the orange patterns of the streetlamps, the roads and lanes and the distant motorway with its hum of night-time lorries.

'My mum's not a pyscho,' I said quietly. 'She's got schizophrenia, that's all.'

'That's bad,' Daniel said after a moment or two.

'You know about schizophrenia?'

'Not really. Just that it's bad. Does that mean you could get it too?'

'What?'

'I mean, through your genes and stuff. DNA.'

'I don't know. I don't think so. I try not to think about it too much.'

'Sorry,' Daniel said.

'Haxforth knows about it. He's got a whole theory, says the mind's like a palace where the king, the person in charge, has been kicked out. You probably think that's a load of rubbish, don't you?'

'No.'

Daniel came and stood next to me, not too close though, and together we stared out at the darkened world. We must've looked like two gargoyles on top of some old church. Down below, three shadowy shapes stepped into the overgrown alley. They walked silent and casual, not aware of being observed. They slid into Christy's van without speaking and drove away.

Haxforth wasn't with them.

'EX05 JYP . . .' I heard Daniel murmur. 'EX05 JYP . . .'

He was tapping at his phone screen again.

'What you doing?'

'Writing down the registration.'

I shrugged. That didn't exactly seem important. How would we ever track it down anyway? It felt stupid, like some TV idea that has nothing to do with reality. If Daniel wanted to play detective though, that was his business.

He slid the phone inside his black coat and we waited, waited, making doubly triply sure they weren't coming back.

Through the hanging door, down the stairs. Telling Daniel to watch out for the leaves and the pigeon droppings. Two torches guiding us because he'd brought one along too. The bolt cutters heavy-balanced in my spare hand. They'd make a good weapon all right, if a weapon was needed.

Breathless now. The blood-drums, instinct, taking over.

Onto the factory floor. The weird-looking machines. The corridor, the canteen where I'd hidden. Next to it the door to the storeroom. The key wasn't even hidden this time, it'd been left in the padlock. I turned it, heard the *click*, saw the bar shoot up.

# 22

It was bad all right, though not easy to tell exactly because of the way he was hunched on the pallet bed. The blankets and coverless duvet were pulled round tight like the last time I'd seen him but now dust and grit lay thick in the fabric folds as if he'd been rolled around on the floor. There was dust clumped too in the dry yellow hair, and his bleached-out eyes were spiderwebbed with scarlet veins. Overall, you had to say he wasn't looking so great.

'It's me,' I whispered. 'Aidan. From before. And this is Daniel . . .'

I shone my torch away, realising I was blinding him. It felt like the coldest place on earth in there, mountain-buried, filled with death. You saw the light beams shining from the torches and you wondered how long till even they froze. I pulled two bananas out of my coat pocket, pinched from the school canteen, a good energy-giving food I knew. Haxforth tore the skins off, squashed them into his mouth. Daniel looked on wide-eyed, breath steaming from his own pale face.

'This is him. The man who gave me the clasp. Didn't you, Haxforth?'

Haxforth nodded, still shovelling banana into his mouth. His teeth were brown and stumpy like half-cooked pieces of popcorn.

'No more messing around,' I said, showing him the bolt cutters.

He felt down around his ankles and yanked the chain out into the open. The way he was huddled, with knees up and arms linked around, it was like he was protecting his stomach. That was the exact same place I'd seen Christy punch him. Maybe there was something else there now. He seemed capable of almost anything, Christy, or at least in my imagination he did. Oh god oh Jesus, I thought, don't let there be any blood or guts spilling out there.

I opened the bolt cutters. Got the chain between the snubby cutting blades while Daniel held the torches. I saw the silver scratch where I'd tried to cut through with the hacksaw. That didn't matter now.

'Go *on*,' Daniel whispered.

I did. I heaved at the bolt cutter's arms and the blade dug in and bit through. Haxforth turned the chain and I sliced the other side of the link and he was free.

'Can you walk?' I said.

'Slowly. Faster without this.'

'Course.' The weight of the pallets was gone, but still there was the tight padlocked loop around his ankle, that part cutting off the blood supply to his foot. I took it slow, not wanting to nick him by accident. But still it was easy. They were magic, those bolt cutters, pure steel magic.

All thanks to Annie Fraser-Howe and her fifty-pound note.

Haxforth rubbed his ankle, tried to stand. It was obvious he needed support, that he couldn't put his full weight on it yet. He was still wearing the same filthy sports gear, the track-suit bottoms, the peeling Reeboks, everything cheap and thin and too big and just what you didn't want to be wearing in the middle of winter. A vicious-looking yellow bruise sprouted up his neck like a diseased sunflower.

He was definitely protecting something, or cradling something, in the front pocket of his grey Admiral hoodie.

More gold perhaps?

'Come on,' Daniel said. 'We need to get out of here.'

'He's right. Can you walk now?'

Haxforth staggered and stumbled towards the door. I grabbed him, got him leaning on my shoulder, got ready to move.

We *did* search for another way out, a ground-floor exit. Christy's way in and out was locked tight as expected so Daniel scouted around and ahead with the torch. Pretty soon though we found ourselves at the bottom of the pigeon-shit staircase. It seemed simplest. Maybe we should've tried harder though. Because choosing the roof, that didn't work out too well at all.

# 23

It wasn't any colder up there than it had been inside. Moonlight showed watery now through the swamp-cloud. I jammed the rooftop door shut behind us, wedged it tight with the bolt cutters. I wanted to put the ghostly world of the Brace Brothers behind me for good.

'Keep moving,' I said to Haxforth. 'Think you can get down a ladder?'

I was worried that if he stopped, his ankle might swell or seize up or something.

'Give me a minute,' he said.

He went and sat on the wide square parapet at the roof's edge, massaging his ankle with one hand, keeping the other protectively around the thing hidden inside the hoodie pocket, whatever it was.

I thought about the clasp, still safe and secure in my pocket.

*If it once kept someone's jewellery in place, what must the jewellery itself have looked like?*

'Aidan.' I felt Daniel's hand tapping at my elbow. 'What are we going to *do* with him?'

'That place on Northcote Road,' I said quietly. 'That homeless place, you know? I thought we'd take him there.'

'They won't be open now! It's too late. Anyway, I don't think you can just turn up, you need to be referred by the council or something.'

'Really?' That blew a big hole in my plans. 'How do you know that?'

'My dad used to volunteer there. I think it was there. That was one of the things him and mum always used to argue about.'

'Used to?' I turned away from Haxforth, still rubbing his ankle, peered at Daniel. The spot on the side of his nose glistened in the weak moonlight and his mouth had crinkled down a bit at the corners.

'I don't really know where he is now. He doesn't live with us any more.'

'Well, I can't take him back to mine,' I said, jerking my thumb at the figure sat over on the parapet. 'I know that much.'

'Why not? You found him.'

'I just can't, all right?' Home was complicated enough already, what with Dad and the mail. No way could I go sliding Haxforth into the picture. 'Let's get him down the ladder and away from this place. We'll work something out after that.'

Daniel didn't say anything, only adjusted his scarf and looked super-serious.

'I'll go first,' I told him. 'Support his legs if I have to. Then you last, how does that sound?'

'What's that he's got in his pocket, do you think?'

I shrugged. 'How should I know?'

'Whatever it is, it's moving.'

'What?'

'That thing in his pocket, that he's protecting. It just moved.'

'You're seeing things.'

I crossed the roof, swung my legs over, lowered myself a few rungs. Right away the frost-knives were biting. The ladder felt like an exposed track now the cloud had thinned and there was more light in the sky. Nowhere to hide once you were on it. So get down fast and safe. Haxforth stood and Daniel manoeuvred him into position and I held up a hand ready to guide his legs.

Down we went, one icy rung at a time. It *had* crossed my mind, sort of, that Haxforth might not have the strength for the climbing and clinging on, but the way I figured it, if you'd been kept prisoner, been starved, you'd take any way out that was available. You'd do whatever it took. He was in a bad way all right but something about him seemed indestructible, like he'd go on forever. But then I guess I'd always thought old people were like that in general, you could never imagine them dying even though you knew they did, that one day their bodies got damaged or diseased and then they stopped working and started rotting instead. Maybe all those assumptions made me a bit casual, I don't know. It wasn't enough to stop what happened next from happening, anyway.

Two-thirds of the way down he fell.

A body crashing into mine and both of us crashing together, that's all I knew. A sickening thud – an earthquake jarring – a body that felt for a minute like mashed potato. Not sure what caused it precisely. A slip, a misjudgement, a moment of muscle weakness, it hardly mattered.

Time did weird skipping jumping things.

'Aidan! Aidan!' Daniel's face hovered large and white, like the moon itself. 'Are you all right?'

'Yeah,' I said. 'I'm OK.'

He pulled me up and I felt all around checking for broken stuff. There wasn't any. I guess I wasn't too far from the ground when Haxforth fell into me. I looked around, saw the bed of tall tangling weeds that'd cushioned my body, saw how my body had cushioned his in turn. Still he'd got the worst of it. We bent down and examined him, Daniel and I. The scarlet veins in his eyes were even worse now and the eyes themselves were rolling like coins that've been spun.

'Oh my god,' Daniel groaned. 'He's bleeding. There, on the side of his head.'

He was right. A dark trickle shone at Haxforth's right temple, drip-dripping into the weeds. Daniel took off his scarf and wrapped it round his hand and pressed it hard to the wound and I thought fair play to him for that, acting like a proper first-aider and everything.

We pulled him forward from the position he'd fallen in and leaned him against the ladder.

'Come on, Haxforth, say something. Tell me some more about those kings and their palaces.'

He mumbled something in response, not proper words though, just odd sounds.

'Look,' Daniel whispered.

Something was definitely wriggling in the front pocket of the grey Admiral hoodie. Even in the fall Haxforth'd protected it somehow, got a thin white hand around it. Now a tiny head poked out. A fierce black eye and a black beak covered around with warts or boils. A neck and body shaking loose from the greasy fabric, ragged feathers fluffing. For a moment it hopped onto Haxforth's shoulder and I saw how the colour on the throat was the same as Haxforth's moonlit blood, matched it exactly. Feebly he made a grab for it but it was away on the wing already.

I remembered then the winter-sheltering bird from the storeroom.

'That was a swallow,' Daniel said. 'Did you see the tail – how it forked?'

'I saw it.'

'But what's it doing here, now? Swallows are summer birds. It should be in Africa or somewhere like that.'

Haxforth was trying to speak, eyelids closed but words clearer this time. I leaned forward, leaned in close to the thin lips and the coffee-coloured tooth-stumps. Daniel did the same.

'All around here . . . There were orchards . . .'

You could tell it was an effort for him, just saying those few words.

'Orchards?' Daniel said. 'What's he talking about?'

He was mysterious all right, Haxforth. Mysterious as a star or an old wild animal. I'd known it right from when I'd first seen him, known it right down in that place where there's no need for words. I was thinking maybe Daniel knew it too, now.

Still, what *were* we going to do with him?

'Do you think he can walk?'

'I don't know. How's his head?'

Daniel dabbed and wiped around with the scarf. 'It seems to be stopping. It's not as deep as it looks. More of a graze.' He wrapped the scarf tight around Haxforth's head like a bandage, put a knot in at the side. 'That should fix it for a while.'

'Great.'

I paced around a bit. I turned on my torch, checking it still worked OK after the fall. Turned it off again straightaway though. There was enough light reaching us from the moon to see by, just about. I curled my fists tight to my forehead, trying to force out a plan, what to do next. Nothing was coming.

'If there was absolutely no other choice . . . I mean, if there was nowhere else at all . . .' Daniel said, looking super-serious again. 'Well, he could stay at mine. Just till morning. We've got a basement with its own front door, down some concrete steps. As long as he's quiet . . .'

'That sounds perfect,' I said, wishing he'd mentioned it before but glad all the same he was doing it now.

'I'm down there a lot, so Mum won't notice anything unusual. I've got my own key and everything. She's sort of let me have it for my own, ever since Dad left.'

I was picturing it in my head already – knowing his road from all those dark-morning mail runs. The history magazines, the stuff my Big Bag carried for D. CUSHWAY. They were massive, those houses. They all had basements and they all went up and up and there were double driveways out the front with brand-new silver cars parked side by side.

'It's near too, Annandale Avenue,' I said without thinking.

'How do you know where I live?'

'What?'

'You said it like you know where I live.'

'Did I?'

'Yeah.'

'Oh,' I said. 'I must've heard it at school or something. Come on. You take that shoulder and I'll take this one.

Haxforth, we're going to carry you – take you somewhere safe. Are you all right with that? Can you walk at all?'

He mumbled something that sounded positive. Or at least didn't sound negative.

We got him under each arm, Daniel and I. Wrestled him up. It felt like he was made out of wire coat hangers. One foot in front of the other and then the other in front of that and then do it again and again.

'He might be concussed,' Daniel said under his breath.

'What do you do for that?'

'I don't know. Lie them down and let them sleep it off?'

I shrugged. I didn't know what you did for concussion either.

Step by step we left the concrete alleyways behind. Flat dark angles, glittering frost, weeds thick and snagging underfoot. They say we're all of us killing nature but it's never seemed that way to me. Give nature five minutes and it comes roaring right back, even the wintertime things that look permanently dead.

'What were you even doing here in the first place?'

'That gang. They nicked my bike and I followed. They were having a laugh.'

Daniel whistled through his teeth. 'I'd've let them have it. They could've been anyone – could've been psychopaths.'

'Just keep moving,' I said. 'Don't break the rhythm.'

# 24

A rainy afternoon sat at the back of the classroom. The cast-iron radiator behind me shovelling out heat. Eyelids heavy. Someone down the front droning on. Everybody bored, everybody watching the clock. Impossible to concentrate anyway, what with being so tired from the night before and thinking over and over how we'd somehow hauled Haxforth across the frozen night-time town and into Daniel's basement – doing our best to keep everything muffled and low noise. Even when we'd got him inside Daniel'd only switched the light on for a minute or two, afraid of drawing attention I suppose. Still I took everything in, like you do when you enter a new room. A big blocky piano, that was the first thing you saw, with an opened book of music, what they call a score, on a little stand above the keyboard. More scores on top of the piano and above those, pinned to the wall, a poster, the Great Composers, faces of men with crazy-mad hair and names and dates underneath.

So I guessed then that Daniel really was some super-whizz at music, like everyone said at school.

There was a faded sofa in there too, patterned with grey geometric shards, something ancient from the 1980s, as well as an electric heater with a red light that flickered when you turned it on. I'd waited a minute or two, helping get Haxforth comfortable on the sofa, but it was obvious Daniel hadn't wanted me to stay. It wasn't like there was anything more to be done anyhow. I'd needed to head home, back to the Big Bag, back to the letters and packets and parcels, everything arranged in street and house order and needing to be delivered fast if I was to stay on top of Dad's stolen mail. Walking away from Annandale Avenue though I'd turned the clasp in my pocket and imagined the look on Christy's face when he discovered the key to his pot of gold had vanished. That made me smile at least.

Down the front, the voice continued its drone. It wouldn't stop. It told us to fiddle about with compasses and protractors and write down formulas in our exercise books. The formulas didn't mean anything to me. I understood them when they were staring up from the page but the minute the page was gone so were they. And what use were they? I was never going to use them outside the classroom. *Nobody* there was ever going to use them.

Then again – people had used maths and stuff to understand DNA, hadn't they? To analyse blood, to figure out the chances of one family member passing something bad on to someone else in the same family. And wasn't that just about the first idea Daniel had had when I'd told him about Mum – how I might inherit her illness? It was scary, that he'd thought it so fast like that. Somehow it made the possibility of me getting sick like Mum seem more real, more likely. The seed had always been there, the fear, cold and buried more or less and not growing too much anyway, but Haxforth had watered it and Daniel had shone some sun down on it and now it was leaping up.

I pushed it away until finally the bells howled and we clattered along corridors. Flickering strip lights and bodies everywhere, open doors and whiteboards, screams and laughter and darkness descending outside. Today's sunlight gone so quickly. End of next week it'll be Christmas.

Last lesson of the afternoon, Miss Tuckett again. I hadn't seen Daniel all day but now there he was, waiting for me by the door.

'He *still* hasn't woken up.'

'What?' I said.

'He still hasn't *woken up*. I thought he'd be gone by now but I went back to check on him at lunchtime and he hasn't moved at all, it's like he's in a coma or something . . .'

I could see he was worried, really worried.

'Keep your voice down,' I said. 'Is he still breathing?'

'Yes, he's breathing but—'

'Come in boys, come in,' Miss Tuckett called from inside the classroom. 'Whatever it is, it can wait till afterwards.'

'He probably just needs loads of sleep,' I whispered. 'Plenty of time to recover . . .'

'That's easy for you to say. You're not the one with a filthy old tramp lying unconscious in your house!'

'He's not an old tramp, he's—'

'Quickly now,' said Miss Tuckett. 'I'm shutting the door. Aidan, have you got your homework?'

'Still haven't done it, miss,' I said.

'Why not?'

'Just haven't.'

The class watched, knowing the routine. The last dragging hour where Miss Tuckett tried to tell us about everything that came before.

'And what about *Beowulf*? Are you going to bother with that? Are you going to read even *one page*?'

She looked determined today, short and steely and determined like she'd finally worked out how to be a proper teacher. 'Are *any* of you going to read it?'

'I've read almost all of it already, Miss Tuckett,' somebody piped up. 'If you like I could—'

Suzanne Dartnell. Class geek, bigmouth, general show-off. Another part of the routine.

'Thank you, Suzanne, but I wasn't asking you,' Miss Tuckett told her sharply.

Suzanne Dartnell pressed her lips together and looked upset.

'Aidan, I want you to come and sit at the front,' Miss Tuckett said. 'Next to Daniel.'

'I don't want to sit at the front,' I said.

'Just do it. In fact I want you to sit there for the whole of next term.'

'That's not fair!'

'Just *do* it.'

Miss Tuckett glared at me. I glared back. Almost standing toe to toe. I knew I'd made her cry in the staffroom before now and I knew I could make her cry again. If I walked out, she'd have to come after me. The thing was, I really did want to know about *Beowulf*, about the kings and witches and monsters that were in it. I *wanted* to learn. About this anyway. Though of course I couldn't ever tell her or anyone else that.

My brain felt hot and angry and totally totally exhausted.

I picked up my bag and my books and moved them to the front row, to the table alongside Daniel, and then I sat down.

'Good,' said Miss Tuckett, blinking, not believing her luck. 'Now, books out and let's begin looking at this ancient poem. The first page, in fact the very first word – 'Attend!' – is really important. Anyone know why?'

Suzanne Dartnell's hand flew up.

'Anyone else?' Miss Tuckett asked hopefully, and when no-one else volunteered she sighed. 'Yes, Suzanne?'

'It shows the poet wanted to be listened to, miss, like he was speaking it instead of writing it down. Lots of these old poems were spoken for years before anybody wrote them down.'

'That's right. Remember what we said about the Dark Ages – about people not writing things down? *Beowulf* belongs to what we call an oral tradition.' Miss Tuckett wrote Oral Tradition in big letters up on the whiteboard. 'So, if people just told the story, why bother to write it down at all? What sort of man, and we think it *was* a man, would do a thing like that?'

'Anybody who could read and write,' someone said.

'Such as?'

'A king?'

'Even a king might not be able to write. A king would probably have had a poem like this read to him, as a form of entertainment. Anyone else? What do *you* think, Aidan?'

Daniel pressed at the fold in the book we were sharing and pointed to a word.

'An atheling,' I said.

'And what's an atheling?' I could hear the surprise in Miss Tuckett's voice.

'Someone from a noble house, miss,' Suzanne Dartnell said.

'Thank *you,* Suzanne!'

'Someone from a noble house,' I said.

'Good *guess,* Aidan. But still not quite right. In fact, it's thought that the story of Beowulf was written down by a priest, an Anglo-Saxon priest, around a thousand years ago. Lots of people have guessed at the exact date, but nobody knows for sure. Make a note of that, please.'

Everyone scribbled down this Important Information.

'Let's read some of it aloud, get a feel for it.' Miss Tuckett smiled, relaxed her shoulders. 'We'll cheat, go to the end, with the dragon. That's the most exciting passage. Storytellers have always saved the best bits till last, even a thousand years ago.'

Then we went around the class, reading out sections of the poem.

A dragon. I didn't know there was one of those in it. Or a thief, who slips into the dragon's lair during the dead of night and steals a golden cup. How Beowulf has to kill the dragon but gets killed himself doing it. How afterwards, as a sort of tribute, the rest of the hoard is buried deep in the ground.

> *They left the earls' wealth in the earth's keeping,*
> *the gold in the dirt. It dwells there yet,*
> *of no more use to men than in ages before . . .*

'But of course,' interrupted Miss Tuckett, 'gold was very useful then, as indeed it is now. It has always been mankind's most valuable metal, and we can see from this poem how it was used to show how rich and important you were. It shines like the sun, so it might have seemed almost magical in the middle of a dark winter. And it never corrodes. You can bury it in the ground and it'll still be there centuries later.' She tapped the book in her hand. 'There are countless examples here of gold casting its spell over men.'

I glanced at Daniel, feeling at the same time the clasp's soft warm metal in my pocket.

The thief. What happened to the thief?

I flicked through the pages ahead but he wasn't mentioned again.

He just seemed to vanish.

# 25

'Who is he, *really*?'

'I don't know. Honest. Everything I know about him, you know too.'

'But he's talked to you, hasn't he? I mean, before. So you must have some idea . . .'

'All right then. It's sort of like he belongs to the past, but somehow he's got loose and ended up here.'

'That's not possible. Or – only in the way that we've all come from the past.'

'I know. But it's what I think anyway.'

We were standing at the school boundary, me and Daniel, right by the blue-and-yellow gates. The sky was darkening and the shadows of homeward bodies teemed under orange streetlamps.

'You're only saying that because of the clasp,' Daniel said. 'Because of what that man told us. But Haxforth could've got it anywhere, he could've stolen it . . .'

'You're right. I reckon that's probably what he did do.'

'Well, that's wrong, if he did. It's just *wrong*. It's against the law.'

I shrugged, started walking. Tried not to think of Annie Fraser-Howe and her fifty-pound note. Daniel kept pace alongside but I didn't want to debate it. I was guessing he didn't know what it was like to be hungry, miss meals, go around with a stomach that kept folding in on itself until you thought maybe it'd disappear altogether like a dried-up puddle.

'You are coming to mine – aren't you?' he said. 'Now, I mean? So we can work out what to do? Only I was really hoping he'd be gone by the time Mum gets back from work.'

'You told me she never goes down there.'

'She doesn't.'

'So what's the problem? If Haxforth's asleep like you say, how will she ever know?'

'He might wake up. I made some jam sandwiches and left them down there for him, and when I went back at lunchtime some of them were gone so I knew—'

I laughed, couldn't help it. 'One minute he's in a coma and the next he's eating jam sandwiches!'

'She just has this way of finding out things,' Daniel said, suddenly miserable.

I looked at him. His face wasn't much more than an outline under the slagheap sky.

'Course I'm coming back to yours. What else did you think I was going to do?'

'Thanks.' I could hear the relief in his voice.

We walked fast through the streets, taking the quickest route to Annandale Avenue.

'What time does your mum get home from work? How

long have we got?' It was a casual question. All I expected was a casual answer.

'I don't know,' he said. 'She's a barrister, usually she works out of town. Tonight I think she's finishing early though. She's on the warpath. That's why I don't want to make her even more angry.'

'Warpath?' That didn't sound good.

'She's got this big case coming up and she's expecting all these important documents in the post. Only they've been lost or something. They haven't arrived anyway. So she's going to the sorting office to make a complaint. She's really angry about it. I think she's got an appointment with the district manager, somebody important like that.' Daniel flashed me an embarrassed look. 'That's something she's really good at, my mum – making a fuss.'

I stopped dead.

'*What?*'

'She's making a complaint, about the post. They were meant to be coming by Special Delivery. It's nothing to do with me.'

'Look,' I said, 'I – I just remembered . . . There's something else I need to do, something important.' In the space of about two seconds everything inside my brain'd got jumbled up, was skidding around. I couldn't get my thoughts in order or find any kind of anchoring point. Daniel stared at me like I'd gone off my head.

'What could be more important than this?'

'I need to – well—'

'But you can't just leave me with Haxforth . . .'

I saw the safe spot then, spied it, made a grab. It was the only thing to do.

'I can get you that post,' I said.

'What?'

'That post – all that post that's gone missing, that your mum's going to complain about – I can get it for you.'

Daniel's mouth opened and shut but no sound came out.

'Seventy-nine Annandale Avenue – that's you, isn't it?'

'Yes, but—'

'Daniel,' I said, 'I'm in really deep shit. I can't explain now but I'll get that post for you – probably by tonight. Only, stop your mum making that complaint.'

'But she might've made it already.'

'Well, call her! Get your phone out and call her and find out and if she hasn't, then stop her!'

I must have looked desperate, standing there practically shaking all over, marble-white from fear most likely and shouting crazy like that.

Daniel didn't move. 'But it's my *mum*,' he said. 'You don't know what she's like . . . What should I say to her?'

'Anything! Anything at all, it doesn't matter. Say – say one of your neighbours got all your post by mistake. And – I don't know – it was sitting all this time in their garage and they were on holiday but now they're back and—'

'But it's all lies!'

'I *know* it's all lies! But I'll get you that post, so it won't matter!'

Still Daniel made no move, no hand towards pocket, no taking out of phone. 'You hit me,' he said. 'You smacked me in the mouth and you made me bleed and you made me give you all that money. Why should I?'

'I know I did. I'm sorry, I'm really sorry. But it's all connected, the money and why I needed it and the post – it's all connected.'

'Tell me then.'

'I can't! Not now! Bloody hell!'

We stood there looking at each other, breath steaming in the cold and the darkness pressing down.

I reached into my pocket. 'Here,' I said. 'It's yours, to keep.'

I held out the clasp. The coiled hinge and the arrowhead catch. You just knew it was really old. It might even be older than the man at the museum said. He was only guessing, after all. He didn't know everything there was to know about history even if he pretended he did.

'How do I know you won't want it back?'

'I won't. It's yours, forever. I promise.'

'My dad made a promise like that,' Daniel said. 'He told me he wasn't going to leave, but he still did.'

'I swear then. On my mum's life.'

'What about Haxforth?'

'One more night?'

Daniel groaned. 'It's a massive risk.'

'Please, please, make that call to your mum.'

Daniel reached out. He took the clasp, turned it over in his hand, the soft warm gold.

I turned, walked away. I couldn't say anything more. I couldn't make Daniel do anything he didn't want to. All that was finished. The mail was the only thing that mattered. Haxforth'd come along and distracted me but he was safe now, more or less. I needed to focus on the things that were real and controllable. Everything else, I had to cut it away, bury it deep.

At the corner I stopped and looked back. Daniel hadn't moved. But his phone was up by his ear and he was talking into it. By the sodium light of a nearby streetlamp I saw him smile, hold an upraised thumb in my direction.

I waved back, then my feet were pounding for home. Out of the pounding came a question:

How many other people were complaining? How many other people were like Daniel's mum, *Really good at making a fuss*?

# 26

I looked in all the rooms to make sure Dad was out, checked from the far end of the garden that none of the neighbours were watching and then I went to open the door of the shed.

It was like an explosion.

Before, the stuff was calf high. I'd been keeping on top of it, or at least that's what I'd thought. I could get inside and wade around and identify the old bundles from the new, the junk mail from the important-looking stuff. Not now. Now it reached over my thighs, flowed out around my knees. I tried to get it back in but it was like pushing water, impossible.

How, why, was there suddenly so much more of it?

All I could think was that maybe Dad had been keeping another stash some place else, some place that wasn't safe any more, and now he'd panicked and moved all of it into the shed. Perhaps that was his idea of taking action.

There was still just enough light to see by. Anyone in the

terrace who happened to look out of their back windows at that moment was going to see a boy and a shed and a mountain of undelivered post. You couldn't miss it or mistake it, the whiteness making it almost fluorescent, lit up somehow from the inside.

I had to act fast. I had to get it out of sight. I ran for the Big Bag, stuffed it full, pelted indoors and up the stairs, dumped the mail in my bedroom. Again and again I did it, five or six times, then I kicked and crammed and shoved and rammed the rest of the mountain back into the shed and somehow got the door shut.

The door that didn't even have a lock.

Up in my bedroom I caught my breath and stirred the mail with my foot like it was some sort of giant cake mix. I climbed over it and sat on my bed and gazed at the condensation on the windowpane.

Even if I found the items for 79 Annandale Avenue, how was I going to deliver all the rest of it?

Bloody hell.

Where *was* Dad anyway? Usually he was back by now, from his pretend job.

I got down on my knees and I started searching.

Adelaide Road, Fremantle Avenue, that pile over there. No point throwing everything into a heap when it all needed to go out anyway. Letters for 3, 4, 12, 16 Fremantle Avenue. A brown jiffy bag for 15 Clarence Villas. Snap decisions, separating out the important stuff. Anything from Pizza Hut or PC World or SpecSavers I shoved to one side. I'd throw those back in the shed tomorrow, try to maximise the floor space in there somehow. Looking all the time for anything with a silver-and-blue sticker on it that said Special Delivery. I'd had a few of those, always made them top priority whenever I saw them, knowing how important they were. Someone had to sign for Specials but I never bothered with that, just shoved them through the letterbox or left them on the doorstep like all the other stuff. People don't care so long as they get their post, that's my experience. Dolphin Way, right down the street, start to finish, letters from the council. The flats on the corner of Mortimer Crescent piled up there –

Bingo. A big padded envelope, a silver-and-blue barcoded sticker, for 79 Annandale Avenue. Daniel's mum's precious documents, standing out a mile. Thank Christ. Keep looking though in case there's more. Letters with scrawled handwriting, neat square birthday cards, letters from the gas and electricity and water and phone companies. Difficult to tell with those which are bills and which are the stupid sales gimmicks. No time to find out even if I wanted to. Another item for 79 Annandale Avenue. And a third, over there. This was more like it.

Hand and eye moving fast, reading, sorting, arranging, not thinking any more.

On and on and on and on and on.

A white envelope, printed, for Ms Annie Fraser-Howe of Flat 6, Langney Place, Totland Terrace.

I stopped. I held it up in front of me, felt the sweat pooling on the tips of my fingers. The pink fifty-pound note I took from her last time, the letter I opened and stole from and then hid behind my fake-wood chest of drawers.

Could there be fifty pounds in this one too?

I turned it over.

I put my thumb under the flap of the envelope. Weak glue, hardly even stuck down at all.

The money I had, the money left over from the bolt cutters, it'd buy school dinners for a while. But it wouldn't last forever.

Give in to temptation. If you've done it once, it's easy to do again.

Almost a habit.

I opened it.

Nothing. No fifty-pound note.

Out of curiosity, I read the letter.

*Rooklands University Hospital*
*NHS Trust*
*Christopher Prince Oncology Centre*
*York Road*

*Dear Ms Fraser-Howe,*

*We are writing to inform you that the results of the tests carried out at the Christopher Prince Oncology Centre on 23 November were, unfortunately, abnormal, and that it will be necessary for us to undertake further investigations. An appointment has been made for you to be seen at the Centre on 19 December at 12:15. Please note that you may be seen by any of the doctors attached to the clinic.*

*Please arrive ten minutes prior to the appointment time to allow your weight and blood pressure to be measured and recorded by the nursing team. Please wear loose-fitting clothes for the appointment and leave any jewellery at home.*

*An abnormal test result may mean many things and there is no reason to be concerned at this stage. For more information we enclose a leaflet, 'Abnormal test results – your questions answered', which also includes contact details of relevant organisations and helplines.*

*As clinic time is valuable, please help us to reduce appointment waiting times by notifying us during normal office hours if you are unable to attend.*

19 December, I thought. That's tomorrow. Doesn't give her much time.

I mean, *Dad* hasn't given her much time.

What's Oncology anyway?

I resealed the letter, ignoring the leaflet, and put it in the stack with the others for Totland Terrace and the streets round about then I packed the Big Bag and grabbed the little pile I'd made up for 79 Annandale Avenue, securing it with one of the red rubber bands they always use at the mail centre.

There was still loads of post I hadn't sorted properly yet so I pushed it under my bed and yanked the quilt down just-got-up-style and decided to have another go at it later.

I went downstairs thinking maybe I'd take five before charging over to Daniel's house. I was feeling pretty wiped out, what with one thing and another. Mrs Cushway had waited all that time for her mail. Another few minutes wouldn't matter, that's how I figured it.

It felt abandoned now, our house. Only the kitchen light was on. The lounge, the little dining area, they were dark and cold. I left them that way. Sometimes when you feel sad and like things are never going to get any better it's OK walking around in the dark. I clicked the TV on and saw an ad for all the fantastic stuff they'd be showing at Christmas. Switched it off right away. Too bright, too cheerful. Christmas wasn't exactly going to be a bundle of laughs this year, what with Mum locked up in Tredegar House with zombie eyes and Dad coming and going whenever he felt like it, getting those sleeping pills off the doctor, not caring about me or him or anyone else.

From a high shelf in the lounge I took down the big red dictionary that lived next door to *A Tale of Two Cities*, which'd somehow ended up in our house. (It'd taken a long time but I'd once followed those pages right through to It Is A Far, Far Better Thing I Do . . .). There was a tiny dead spider on top but that was new because I took it down quite often, the dictionary, liking to look up words I didn't know. I carried it through to the lighted kitchen, brushed off the spider, turned and scanned the pages.

> ***oncology*** *n the study of tumours*
> ***oncogene*** *n a type of gene involved in the onset and development of cancer.*

I felt numb all over.

Annie Fraser-Howe had cancer and she didn't even know it because my dad was too lazy to get off his arse and do his job.

Annie Fraser-Howe who I stole fifty pounds off.

Annie Fraser-Howe whose hospital appointment was tomorrow at 12.15.

I stood there a long time, staring at those words. I don't know how long exactly. They had a mesmerising sort of power. I only stopped when I heard the gate outside click open, when I heard footsteps coming down the path.

I ghosted across the kitchen and pressed myself to a wall where they wouldn't see me, whoever it was.

*Knock knock knock.*

'Bob? You in there? Bob?'

*Knock knock knock.*

'Answer the door! It's Hawkie. I need to talk to you.'

*Bang bang bang.*

'Listen, this is serious. I was talking to Eric and he was talking to Danny. An email got forwarded by mistake, from Investigations. Bob, they're monitoring you . . .'

*Bang Bang Bang.*

'You're an idiot! A bloody idiot! Anyone ever tell you that?'

Hawkie knocked once more and then he swore and sighed and went away.

After that I did a really funny thing. I went and put my hands in the greasy sink. I pushed them right down into the icy water. At the bottom there was a whole load of dirty knives and forks, a whole sharp dirty frozen load. I picked them up in my hands and tightened my grip, tightened and tightened and tightened. It hurt like hell at first but pretty soon all the feeling went away and then it was better. Having my eyes screwed shut the whole time, that helped too.

# 27

79 Annandale Avenue. The double driveway, the iron railings and half-hidden basement off to one side, the five steps leading up to the big front door. I propped the racing bike against the hedge and took out the rubber-banded package from inside my coat. What I really wanted to do right then was go sneaking down those basement stairs to check on Haxforth. It felt too risky though, what with all the windows lit up and the big silver car out there on the drive. Even knocking on the front door to deliver Mrs Cushway's mail might be taking too much of a chance. What if she answered, and not Daniel? No, I'd drop it quietly through the letterbox, the brass-edged brushless letterbox that I knew already, and be on my way. If there was any news about Haxforth, Daniel'd just have to tell me about it in school tomorrow.

I went up the steps and started putting the stuff through but even as the first package hit the mat the door was opening.

'I didn't know if you'd come,' Daniel said, looking relieved. It was like he'd been standing there that whole time. Then, 'Blimey, Aidan, you look terrible.'

'Here you go.' I thrust the rest of the mail into his hands. 'I think that's all of it. It's all I could find anyway.'

'Where'd you get it from?'

I shrugged the question away. 'How's Haxforth?'

'Sssh!' Ask me about that later, Daniel was saying. Not *now*.

'What's that whispering?' a voice called from the far end of the hall. 'Come into the kitchen. You're letting all the warm air out.'

Daniel took the post I'd delivered and put it on a shelf in the hallway, arranged it beside some other bits of paper and envelopes and takeaway menus, and then he motioned for me to follow him inside.

It seemed to be made completely of metal, the kitchen of 79 Annandale Avenue. There was a boxlike metal island in the middle of the tiled floor and above it a metal cage hung with shiny metal pots and pans. The cupboards were metal and there was a great metal hood over the metal cooker and it was big and clean and coffee was brewing somewhere among all the silver gadgets. I thought of my kitchen, of the cold brown water, the shrivelled apple, the red bill from the gas company.

'And who's this?'

Daniel's mum. Mrs Cushway. She was standing beside the metal island, glossy bags, the sort you get from expensive clothes shops, piled up around high-heeled feet. Everything about her looked brittle and no nonsense.

'Mum, this is Aidan. Aidan, Mum.'

'Pleased to meet you, Aidan.'

She didn't look pleased to meet me, though. She looked like she was already counting the minutes till I got out of her house.

'Oh,' Daniel said casually, 'I forgot to tell you. All that stuff you were waiting for? It came about half an hour ago.'

'Well, why on earth didn't you tell me? Where is it?'

'Out there.'

Mrs Cushway disappeared, came back a moment later with those items that until a short time ago'd been lost inside Dad's shed. Her lips were puckered and white. 'You *know* how important these documents are,' she said. 'You *know* tomorrow's the first day at Winchester. Really, Daniel, I wonder what goes on inside your head sometimes.'

Daniel turned, about to walk away.

'And you still haven't explained yourself,' Mrs Cushway continued, like there hadn't been any break in the conversation. 'I haven't heard you practising today. Or yesterday. Is there a problem?'

'The piano's out of tune . . .' Daniel said, not too convincingly.

'It can't be. The man only came last month. Hours he spent, plinking away down there. I'm afraid it sounds rather like an excuse to me.'

'It's not an excuse . . .'

'All we want is the best for you, darling,' Mrs Cushway said, a little softer. 'Once your friend's gone, I really think you ought to go downstairs and have another try at the Beethoven.'

I looked at Daniel, wanting to know what he'd have to say to *that*. But then I looked away, seeing how his face was big and burning suddenly and his eyes glued to the floor.

'There's no need to be a baby about it,' she said. 'Really.' From one of the silver machines she poured out a cup of coffee, and then she gathered up the glossy shopping bags and the padded envelopes. 'Well, I'm going upstairs. I need to get to work on these right away. There are pizzas in the freezer. Just remember what I said. In the New Year they'll be expecting you to practise *at least* two hours a day . . .'

'Perhaps I should go?' I said, taking a step back into the hallway.

'Hang on. Just wait in there a minute.' Daniel pointed me towards another door that led away from the kitchen, into what seemed like a lounge. 'That's OK, isn't it?'

'Not for too long, I think,' Mrs Cushway said. 'I'm sure Aidan will need to be home before it gets too cold.'

I stepped from the large kitchen into a room with an enormous sofa, a wooden dining table, two crystal chandeliers, a wall of books and a fireplace. It was real, this fireplace, with tongs and a scoop and a brush hanging in a brass stand off to one side. They were all dusty though and so was the iron grate. There hadn't been a fire there in ages. I thought what a shame that was, how nice it would've been to crouch down and rub my hands in front of real flames, feel the heat while outside the nightly frost settled. When Daniel didn't come I went over to the bookcase and looked along the shelves.

The top shelf had a lot of big textbooks with titles like *The Law of Criminal and Civil Evidence*. Beneath that there were flat-stacked art books and some green paperbacks, novels, I guessed, though I'd never heard of any of them. All the rest were history-type things with important-sounding names like *God's Englishman* and *The Pursuit of the Millennium*.

Right at the bottom, in a corner, was a copy of *Beowulf.* I took it out and went and sat down on the sofa.

> *A boat with a ringed neck rode in the haven,*
> *icy, out-eager, the atheling's vessel,*
> *and there they laid out their lord and master . . .*

It was a beautiful thing to look at and hold, a heavy hardback with gold lettering on the cover, the paper inside rough and grainy in a nice kind of way. The Old English printed on the left-hand pages with the translation facing them. Those weird angular runes, they could mean anything. How had anybody ever made sense of them? How did everyone else know they got it right?

Daniel appeared at the door. He shut it behind him. He sat down next to me on the sofa. I thought his face was still red but I didn't like to look too close. Mrs Cushway seemed to have gone upstairs.

'Thanks for pointing out that word to me,' I said. '"Atheling." That old bag of a teacher . . .'

'What am I going to *do?* He was meant to be gone by now.'

I didn't know what to say. I was feeling pretty bad about Daniel's situation, that was the truth. I mean, I hadn't forced him to take Haxforth in or anything but still at the same time I felt sort of responsible.

'Can't we go downstairs and check on him?' I said. 'That's what she wants you to do isn't it – go down to the basement?'

'We'll have to. But give it a few minutes, let her get properly stuck into her work.'

'All right.'

I turned the pages of the book, still in my lap. Something was written in blue ink on the inside front cover, there in the top right corner:

*Dennis Cushway, Berkeley, California.*
*May 1979.*

So then I knew who the D. CUSHWAY was who I'd been delivering all the history stuff to.

Daniel glanced across. 'Take it,' he said.

'What?'

'Take it. Keep it. You gave me Haxforth's clasp. So you have that.'

'But it belongs to your dad . . .'

'He isn't coming back for it. He isn't coming back for anything that matters.'

'Oh,' I said.

Silence. One of those uncomfortable sound-emptinesses you want to break but somehow all it does is feed on itself.

I gazed some more at the *Beowulf* pages. Not just the proper English and the sense you could get out of it but the ancient impossible facing words. I thought of what Miss Tuckett said. Try to imagine the life of the person who first wrote it down. Try to believe what they believed.

'Where'd you get that post from, Aidan?'

I looked at Daniel. He already knew about Mum, how she'd been sectioned. And he'd sheltered Haxforth in his basement despite not really wanting to. Now under the crystal chandeliers I told him the rest of it – about the mail Dad brought home and how I'd been trying to deliver it to keep him out of trouble, and about Matthew Greenwood from Birmingham who got fourteen months in prison for doing the exact same thing, and about the men at Royal Mail whose job it was to monitor and watch and investigate.

It took about ninety seconds to tell. Less, even. Funny how something so massive can come out so fast. Sort of like a missile being fired. You can feel the hole where it's been, too.

'And that's why you needed your bike?' he said, when I'd finished talking.

I nodded.

'They really send people to jail for that?'

'Yeah. And if they do, if Dad gets sent down and Mum's still in hospital, guess where I'll end up?'

'Where?'

'Care home.'

Daniel stared into the cold grey fireplace. 'At least you try to do something about your problems,' he said. 'I just curl up and pretend mine aren't happening. Or pretend they're happening to someone else, not me.'

Another minute or two passed in silence.

'You know, if there was any more post for Annandale Avenue, I could – well – help you with it. If you wanted me to, I mean.'

'Yeah?'

'Yeah. Mum won't be around much in the next few days. She's so caught up in this trial . . .'

'There's loads more,' I said, closing *Beowulf* and putting it on a little coffee table-type thing. 'It's endless.'

'That's all right. What time do you start?'

'4.30. A bit before, usually.'

His eyes bulged at that, but still he nodded OK.

I was going to say thanks only just then, down in the

basement, something crashed over. A loud metallic ringing crashing that seemed to echo through the whole house.

Instantly we were on our feet, staring at each other, alert like gazelles.

# 28

We listened hard for a long minute. No reaction from upstairs.

'Sometimes she puts earphones in when she's working,' Daniel whispered.

Fast and soft we slipped outside, Daniel telling me how he'd made sure the internal door to the basement was locked tight, with his mum believing the key to be lost. Down the iron-railinged steps, then through a windowless unfriendly door which Daniel secured behind him immediately, following procedure, security-conscious above all else.

It was dark in there and hot and it didn't smell too good, sort of like an animal's lair. A moment of fumbling and then a small pink table lamp went on and we saw Haxforth. He was down on the floor. His face looked white like flour but that didn't mean anything because I'd only ever seen it that colour, it wasn't like he'd once had apple-red cheeks and now this. I guessed the bright smears around his mouth were from all the jam sandwiches Daniel'd been leaving him.

'Haxforth! You're awake!'

He stared at us. The sports gear needed burning but apart from that he didn't look too bad. The blood from the cut on his head had dried out and there were some black scab-fragments matting the thin yellow hair. His eyes were pale again, the pure and non-diluted colour of winter, if winter has a colour. He was trying to pick up the heavy upright heater, one of those things like radiators only you move them around on little wheels. It'd fallen over hitting the piano, and that was what made the crashing ringing noise.

'You're the one who came with the cutters,' he said slowly, 'who thinks like a peasant.'

'We *rescued* you. Me and Daniel here. This is Daniel's house we're in now. And I'm not a peasant.'

'No. Aidan – that's your name, isn't it?'

I nodded.

'Well, Aidan. And Daniel. This is wonderful. I don't believe it's meant to fall over though.'

I knelt down to help. 'It's just a heater,' I told him.

'Feel it.'

I touched it – had to while I hauled it upright. It was red hot.

'Fantastic,' Haxforth said. 'The trouble is, it burns the skin after a while.'

'Yeah,' I said. 'You have to watch out for that.'

'I've been so cold, so right-down-deep-in-the-earth cold.'

'How are you feeling?' Daniel asked.

'My head hurts.' Gingerly Haxforth rubbed at his scalp.

'I'm not surprised. It was quite a way you fell. You remember that – falling off the ladder?'

'It's all a blur . . . I hardly know how I came to be here . . .'

We lifted him onto the sofa with its pattern of grey geometric shards. He'd made a nest there similar to the one back in the Brace Brothers factory.

'But you remember the other place, being chained up?'

'Oh yes, I remember *that*. The bruises remind me, should I ever forget.'

I thought, We can't send him away like this. Not with Christy and his sick little gang still out there, even more vicious now knowing somebody must've helped him escape, wanting revenge and retribution.

'There was a bird,' Haxforth said. 'Have you seen a bird?'

'We saw something, but it flew away. A summer swallow?'

'That's it. He came to me, through the broken windows. Only there was the chain around my ankle, stopping me from going with him . . .'

'Going with him?' Daniel said. 'Where?'

Haxforth stared up at the ceiling. One of those glazed-over looks where you know the person isn't in the present any more, they're in the past, or thinking deeply about it anyway.

'You can tell us,' I said softly. 'You're safe here.'

I meant it, too. Somehow the solid upright slab of piano, and the heat and the pink glow from the table lamp, which was exactly the same colour you see in photos of womb-growing babies, made this place, the basement at 79 Annandale Avenue, seem like the safest place on earth. I don't know why that should be, it was more feeling than fact because after all Mrs Cushway could come prowling any moment. But somehow the room felt sealed-off and separate so I understood why Daniel'd felt he could take the risk, bringing him here in the first place.

Haxforth smiled. Ghostly yes but not completely broken down. 'I'm someone who had to go away. The time's come to return home. I couldn't before – only now.'

'But where are you actually trying to *get to*?'

'A place called Shuttle Hill. It's near here, very near. That's where I was going when I ran into Christy and his friends.'

'What happened?'

'It was on a path I was using. A wide path, with tyre tracks in the mud. That should've warned me. They were sorting through the back of their van. The way the path turned – the trees that were there – I ran right into them.'

'And that's when they found the bracelet?' I said.

Haxforth nodded. 'One of them must have caught a glimpse as I tried to go past. They had it off me in seconds – demanded to know where I'd got it from. Someone shoved me . . . I remember stumbling, falling. Babbling something or other. I must have passed out. The trouble was, I hadn't eaten in a long while, not properly. It was easy for them. The next thing I knew the doors of the van were slamming shut and everything was going dark . . .'

'But they didn't get the clasp?'

'No. I had that well hidden. There were some places even they didn't want to search.'

'Where *did* you get them from?'

'The houses of the rich.'

We sat in silence for a minute, me and Daniel. Haxforth had closed his eyes and I thought maybe he was drifting off again, back to sleep. I looked at him, wondered who he really was and where he'd come from. The strange thing was, I got the feeling that even if he told us it would still explain nothing. He could talk for an hour and still be full of mysteries I'd never fathom. People are like that in general, you never know what they're thinking, not deep in their own invincible hearts. Well, Haxforth, he was like that too, only a hundred or a thousand times *more*.

'And when you get to this place,' I said quietly, trying to press him, 'Shuttle Hill or whatever it's called, that's where there'll be somewhere for you to stay? And someone who'll look after you? Because, you know, you can't really stop here any more.'

Haxforth nodded. Eyes still closed. 'That's where he is. My brother. All ready to take me in.'

'Your brother who heard voices in his head?' I heard my own voice tighten, saying it. I hadn't forgotten any of that stuff he'd told me back in the Brace Brothers factory. 'Who you said you helped once?'

'That's right. Once.'

Daniel glanced at me. 'Maybe we can find it on a map,' he suggested. 'There're loads upstairs. Dad used to have a thing about them, especially old ones.'

'I don't think you're going to find it on any map.'

'Has he got a car? We could call him, get him to come and pick you up. If it's not too far.'

'No.' Haxforth's eyelids looked like two white chocolate buttons in their stillness and waxiness. 'No car. He's not too mobile these days.'

'He'll be able to look after you OK though?' I said. 'When you're there?'

'Oh yes. When I'm there. But not without the bird. Not without Old Beautiful.'

'Old Beautiful?'

Daniel tapped me on the arm, pointed at the ceiling. His

antennae alert and switched on high. Mrs Cushway was walking about upstairs, short clipped steps, still wearing those high heels.

'You've got to promise to be *quiet*. You're not supposed to be here at all, see. If Daniel's mum finds you . . .' I drew a finger across my throat, indicating Sudden Death.

'Quiet as a summer cloud, that's me,' Haxforth whispered.

Jesus Christ he looked old. All the things he must have seen and all the things he must have done. Was he asleep now? Old men are like little babies in some ways. They sleep and sleep and then sleep some more. With babies, they're sleeping because they need to get ready for life. Maybe with old men they're sleeping to get ready for the other thing, the thing that happens to all of us in the end.

Up above I heard the front door open. The short clipped steps were outside, moving with intent. Daniel looked at me panicked. We both knew they were going to turn at the iron railings that led down to the basement room.

He killed the light and in a flurry we were closing the door behind us and trying to get out.

'Oh,' Mrs Cushway said, seeing me from the top of the basement steps. '*You're* still here.'

'Aidan's just leaving,' Daniel said loudly.

'I didn't hear you practising. Why not? Mr Gillessen says that to have any chance of . . .'

'I was practising the adagio,' Daniel said. 'Soft pedal. *Pianissimo.* So it wouldn't make much noise, would it?'

Mrs Cushway looked confused.

'It was very beautiful,' I said.

'Yes. Well – anyway. I wanted to check, that's all.'

Daniel shot me a look. You better go now, it said.

I edged down the driveway and pulled the racing bike out of the hedge. It was obvious Mrs Cushway wasn't going to let me stay there another moment longer. If anything happened here tonight with Haxforth, Daniel was just going to have to deal with it on his own. Walking away down Annandale Avenue, wheeling the bike, I heard her say, 'Ridiculous, having to come outside in the cold like this! We need to find that key.'

I don't suppose I could've stayed too much longer anyway. It was time to get home, time to haul and heave the mail in my secret practised way. Time to get sorting again. The moon would be out tonight, almost full – not that the alliance would mean much if the cloud stayed so thick in the sky. Only, moving through the dark streets, I felt this *idea* growing inside. An idea that made my stomach tip and roll the more I thought about it.

Perhaps, before he disappeared, there was something Haxforth could do to help *me*.

It was so stupid. Just because he had a brother who'd heard voices, once, in the past, and now he didn't hear them any more. There could be any number of reasons for that. I mean, what exactly did I expect to happen? It was stupid, pointless, a fantasy. But deep down, deep down and in secret, I really was thinking, If *once* why not *again*?

I did the right thing though. I squashed that idea out of existence, before it grew big enough to hurt me later on.

# 29

4.10, the red lights of the digital clock said. The dream was hovering right inside my forehead, the dream where I tried to run from the collapsing houses of mail while the Queen stared at me with enraged eyes. This time there'd been a new twist. That woman with the Oncology letter, Annie Fraser-Howe, she'd been floating somewhere alongside. She was a pale rotting mushroom with postage stamps for eyes and nose and mouth. She wanted to tell me something but the stamps were thick and solid and they acted like corks in a bottle, stopping anything from coming out.

I lay in the warm bed, forced the images away. They weren't relevant. Be like a machine, I told myself, a perfect machine.

The trouble is, machines don't dream, do they? When they're off, they're off. Whereas when *I'm* off, there's still something going *on*.

Then I remembered about Dad and that did the job all

right, killing off the nightmare. Last night he hadn't been in the house at all. Or at least not when I'd laid down to go to sleep. I'd carried and sorted another load of mail, got it all ready and ordered with the Big Bag empty but waiting at the foot of the bed, and nowhere in that time had Dad been around.

Where was he?

I pulled on jeans, jumpers, trainers, armour-plating against the cold, went from room to room, flashing the torch that always seemed to be with me now. Nothing. Nobody had been there in all the hours I'd been asleep. Every room silent, every corner cold and void-like. A house carved from a giant ice cube.

I thought again of Hawkie, shouting through our front door about Dad being monitored at work. I thought of Mrs Cushway and her undelivered post. If *she'd* been angry enough to complain, how many others were there feeling the same way? Loads probably. And even though I'd tried so hard to be secret and silent, perhaps some of them had seen me out with the Big Bag and put two and two together. I imagined all these people asking questions, making demands. Busybodies. There're busybodies everywhere, making wheels spin faster. Just because I couldn't see them, those wheels, it didn't mean they weren't turning. I might not see them *at all* until the moment they rolled right down on top of me.

Yes. That was it. Dad had seen them too and he'd done a runner. Just upped and gone. Left me on my own and Mum in Tredegar House.

He wouldn't do that, would he?

Yes.

No.

Don't know.

For a few minutes it was about all I could do to stand there in the dark and remind myself over and over that a person can't be killed by cold crushing panic.

Back to the bedroom window, to check the weather. I needed to stay focused, keep doing all the things I'd been doing up till then. My sleeve rubbed at the windowpane. Outside I saw a crystalline frost thickening the surface of the world.

And something else.

There, huddled under the streetlamp, in the exact same spot as the scumbag pair who'd stolen my bike, stood Daniel Cushway.

I ran out and beckoned him inside. He had a bike of his own, propped against a nearby wall, which he wheeled into the passageway while I dulled the squeaking gate. I don't know how he knew where I lived. Maybe he found it on the internet. You can find out pretty much anything on that these days, if you have a connection.

'I couldn't sleep,' he whispered. 'Worrying about stuff. So I thought I'd come and help you. 4.30, that's what you said.'

'What about your mum?'

'I should be OK if I'm back by seven.'

I saw how he'd brought a rucksack too, for carrying the mail.

'Come inside. Get warm for a minute, before we start.'

It felt stupid, walking around my own house in the dark now someone else was there. Up in the bedroom I flicked on the light switch and scooped the mail out from under the bed.

'Where's your dad?' Daniel said nervously.

'I don't know. He didn't come home last night.'

'Really?'

'Yeah, really.'

Daniel watched me arranging the bundles, saying nothing, all stony and serious like a churchyard statue.

'How much more of it is there?' he said at last. 'You told me your dad puts it in his shed.'

'There's tonnes. This is just a little part of it.'

Daniel whistled softly. 'Come on then, give me some. Not just Annandale Avenue. More than that.'

'Thanks, Daniel.'

I passed him one bundle, another, another, told him the street names, the directions he should take and the order he should do everything in. All that stuff came easy now, easy as dreaming.

We stowed everything in the bags, got them shouldered.

'There's something I've sort of been thinking about,' Daniel said, a bit cautious and delaying.

'What's that?'

'The clasp. Do you reckon I should ask him about it?'

Daniel hadn't mentioned Haxforth till then so I'd assumed he was still safe in the basement at 79 Annandale Avenue.

'Don't know. Where is it now?'

Daniel patted at a square shape in his pocket. 'I've put it in a matchbox, wrapped it in toilet roll to protect it.'

'Do what you like. It belongs to you, doesn't it?'

'What if he wants it back? I mean, he seems to have forgotten, but if I say something it might remind him.'

'Then don't ask. Keep quiet.'

'But if I keep it and deliberately don't say anything – well, it's not right, is it? It's stealing, basically.'

I rolled my eyes. 'Every thief for himself,' I said.

'What?'

'"Every thief for himself." Something he said to me when I first found him.'

'But I'm not a thief.'

We went down the stairs and Daniel waited in the kitchen while I fetched the key to unlock the racing bike. The clock on the microwave said 04.39.

'Something that old – it must've been through hundreds of hands,' I told him.

Daniel looked unhappy at that but what did he expect? It wasn't like I was a schoolteacher, telling people what to do and how to behave.

We left the house, cycling past silent cars white-windscreened from the frost. Past the faded tubes of the play park at the end of the Crescent where I'd jumped and tumbled as a little kid. No moon tonight. It was up there, a sliver off being fully round, only shut behind armies of cloud.

'You know that big place on Willowfield Road, all covered in scaffolding?' I said – whispered, since in the dead of night even quiet voices sound like loudspeakers at midday.

'Yeah.'

'Let's meet there, in ninety minutes. See how we're getting on.'

'OK.'

I watched his back disappear into the dark. He was wobbling slightly from the weight of the mail but I had to assume he'd be all right. I'd asked for the help, after all – in a roundabout sort of way.

I knew deep down that it couldn't go on forever. Of course I knew. Whether it was Hawkie's investigators, or some random casual complaint, or some other thing I couldn't foresee or imagine, this never-ending task was going to end some day soon.

That day wasn't today though.

I gathered myself in, knowing time goes faster that way. I had to move like clockwork, be the perfect machine, not let myself get distracted. There'd been too much of that recently.

I checked the first bundle, then I started pedalling.

The very top letter was addressed to Annie Fraser-Howe.

# 30

Ninety minutes later, plus some, loitering outside the big gutted house on Willowfield Road.

Where was he?

I'd given him too much. I knew that now. What'd I been thinking? He didn't know the route like I did, didn't know the individual houses or the awkward unnumbered flats, didn't know how to go invisible through the night like me. And now night was almost over, grey in the sky, signs of an approaching sun.

I reached for the rusting racer, propped there against the scaffolding. Then I put it back. I didn't know whether to stay or go. It wasn't good, all this hanging around. My stress levels were swamping up a bit. I should be finishing now, thinking about it at least, heading home, getting off the streets.

The minute you trust someone you're asking to be let down, that's my experience.

Then I saw him away in the distance. It was light enough to see that. From the way his rucksack was flapping I knew most of the mail had gone. He was riding pretty fast, knowing he was late probably, needing to get home before that dragon-thing that called itself his mother woke up.

His bike skidded to a halt in front of the scaffolding. 'EX05 JYP!' he said. 'EX05 JYP!'

'What?'

'Christy's van! I saw it! Parked outside a house on the Cloisters.'

'You sure?'

'Yeah. I had to go back that way and I saw it twice. The same one we saw from the roof of that old factory, definitely.'

I shivered inside. The Cloisters was right on the boundary of Dad's route, not too far from home. I didn't like the thought of Christy being so near. Perhaps it wasn't so surprising though, it being a small town and always bumping into people whether you wanted to or not.

'Well, that's one bastard who won't be getting any more mail.'

'But what are we going to *do*?' Daniel said excitedly.

It was funny, the way he was looking and talking at me, like I was the one in charge, a general ready with strategies and schemes. But I didn't feel general-like at all. I was tired, exhausted – felt more like a bankside fish smacked on the head, waiting for the angler's knife.

'Do? Nothing.'

'But you were the one who—'

'What do you *want* to do? Go and slash his tyres just when his neighbours are getting up for work?'

'No, of course not, but—'

'How did you get on with the mail?'

Daniel looked disappointed. He was all revved up, proud of his discovery, wanting to jump feet first into action. He opened the bag, showed it to me. Empty – completely empty. Not one single item left.

Something happened then I wasn't expecting. Something inside, I mean. I don't know where it came from. There I was, acting all tough, like a general after all maybe, and the minute I saw the inside of that empty bag I practically burst into tears. It was totally pathetic. I was just so grateful he'd done it, that was the thing.

'That's really helped,' I mumbled.

'I'll do it again tomorrow, if you want.'

'Great.'

We stood there and I didn't say anything and he didn't either so it was turning into one awkward moment when suddenly Daniel's coat started ringing. We both jumped about a foot in the air. It sounded like a siren in the morning quiet, like the loudest thing you'd ever hear. He fumbled, took it out, the same top-of-the-range handset I'd threatened to hurl from the Brace Brothers rooftop. I saw him check the number, go pale.

'Hello?' he said timidly.

I could hear the voice at the other end. The drone of an angry insect – a queen bee.

'But –' pleaded Daniel. 'But I – yes. No, no, I'm fine . . . Is there? No, I didn't – Well, just out. Aidan's here . . .'

That went on for a few seconds. Then he hung up. His face was all white and his lips were shaking.

'Who was it?' I said, like I didn't know.

'Mum. She says there's a disgusting old man in the house.

He's frying bacon in the kitchen, and unless I get home in two minutes flat to explain to her where I am and what's going on, she's dialling 999.'

'Oh *shit*,' I said.

# 31

Never have I seen anyone ride a bike like Daniel did then. The sprint sections of the Tour de France had nothing on it. He reached Annandale Avenue first though I wasn't far behind because I can do speed too if I need to, it's not all stopping and starting and lugging the Big Bag.

I don't really know what I was expecting to see but there he was, Haxforth, sitting on the bottom-most of the five steps leading up to the front door. We threw our bikes against the basement railings. Mrs Cushway was standing beside the big silver car wearing a blue business suit. Her hair was done and her teeth were white and she looked ready to go out and earn lots and lots of money. Looked, when I thought about it, like the sort of person who'd put my Dad behind bars and call it a Great Victory.

'I want you –' she pointed at Daniel – 'to tell me what has been going on *in my own house* and who the hell *he* is.'

'That's Haxforth.' Daniel's voice trembling as he said it.

'Oh well, that explains *everything*, doesn't it?'

Haxforth opened his hands wide and smiled apologetically. He looked like a collection of bones held together by dirt and rags. 'I suddenly felt ravenous,' he said. 'I thought the house was empty.'

'He's been sleeping down there, hasn't he? I've seen the mess. It's *foul*. Like some – some place where junkies go. No wonder I haven't heard you practising. What on earth were you thinking? And what will your father say, when I tell him?'

'He won't care,' Daniel said quietly.

'I beg your pardon?'

'Nothing.'

'I have *no idea*, Daniel, what could have possessed you to let somebody like – like *that* – into our house, but believe me I will be getting to the bottom of this when I get back. Just consider yourself lucky that I'm in such a hurry. In fact I'm late already, thanks to you. Do you know, really, how *big* this case is? Do you know *how far* I have to drive this morning? Do you know *anything* about what I have to deal with now that your father's gone?'

Daniel seemed to be curling under the onslaught. Something about the angle of his head reminded me of those films you see where they strap a dummy into a car and then drive it into a wall to see how a real human body will deal with the impact. Then she turned on me. That was OK though, better in some ways since I'm no crash-test dummy but someone who can hold their neck straight and butt right back at anything coming their way.

'This is all your fault,' she said. '*You*—'

'Aidan,' I said.

'Yes, Aidan.' (She said it like something she'd seen writhing wet and pale through the soil at the bottom of her garden.) 'It's people like you, sending him off the rails like this. He was perfectly all right until you came along – you and that – that *tramp*.'

I thought, No, he wasn't perfectly all right at all, not that you'd ever think to listen and understand about it.

'And that wretched school. Nothing but trouble from beginning to end. The music department is a joke. Lessons in rapping! Well, thank heavens it's your final week, Daniel.'

I glanced over at Daniel but he wasn't making eye contact with anything except the little pieces of gravel on the driveway. He seemed to be examining those individually and in great detail.

'Final week?' I said to him.

'Oh yes,' Mrs Cushway said. 'After Christmas – new term, new school, new start. Linden College. Frankly I would have got you in there earlier, much earlier, if it wasn't for your father and his peculiar ideas about education.'

I didn't know too much about that place, Linden College. Just that it was out of town, with cricket grounds the size of aircraft runways and a sort of church thing of its own, and that parents paid for their kids to go there.

'It's all arranged. Piano lessons with Mr Gillessen. You're incredibly lucky to get someone of his—'

'What about him?' Daniel mumbled. He pointed at Haxforth, still sitting on the bottom step but gazing now at a dead stump of tree hemmed into the far concrete corner. He didn't seem to have the first idea about the trouble he'd caused.

Mrs Cushway flashed her iron-sentinel eyes from Haxforth to Daniel and back again. She reached into the jacket pocket of her business suit and took from a tiny leather purse a ten-pound note. 'Oh *god*,' she said to Haxforth. 'Just take this. Use it to go to a cafe or something. And you, Daniel, I want you to come inside and clean up the basement. Blitz the place. I've put cream cleaner and bleach on the kitchen top. Make sure you use rubber gloves when you use the bleach, you know you have to be careful with your hands . . .'

Daniel puffed out his cheeks. He moved towards the house, all lowdown and obedient.

Haxforth was still staring at the scrawny tree. Lost in his own world, drifting off. Precious lot of use *that* was.

'Now I have to go. Frankly I'm in shock. I'm starting to wonder, Daniel, if there isn't a need for you to see someone. Someone who can help you get back on track, stop all this strange behaviour. *I* certainly don't understand it anyway.' Mrs Cushway unlocked the car, climbed in. 'Heaven knows I wouldn't be going unless I absolutely had to.'

She backed out and drove away.

After that nobody spoke for a couple of minutes. I looked up at the sky. Daylight was here, not that you could call it that, a murky glow more like. Boiler-steam spouted up and down Annandale Avenue, houses warming themselves from the long winter night.

'You didn't tell me you were leaving St Stephen's,' I said.

Daniel shrugged. He still didn't want to look at me, and who could blame him?

I nodded at Haxforth and the banknote he was holding in his hand.

'We could all go together . . . have a fry-up . . .'

'Better not.' Daniel went up the steps to the front door.

'Thanks,' I said.

'What for?'

'For – you know. Helping with the mail. Coming with me to that place in the middle of the night.'

'No problem.'

'It was great, how we ran out of the museum like that.'

'Yeah.'

He went inside, pulled the door behind him till all I could see was a narrow strip of face and body.

'See you around, then.'

'Yeah. See you around.'

The door closed with a quiet metallic *click.*

'Well done,' I said, turning to Haxforth. The ten-pound note had blown out of his hand, was drifting into the road on a little breeze that'd blown up. I ran and caught it. *Nobody* lets something like that sail away.

'The tree,' he whispered. 'Look.'

I looked. He meant the black stunted thing in the corner, the one with the trunk all covered in sickly fungus and the branches like smashed TV aerials.

Slowly, slowly, the fungus was peeling away. It spiked up like a lawn in summer and dried and separated from the bark and then it fell to the concrete. The bark itself seemed to be changing colour. The black was gone, the slick unhealthy black, replaced by a powdery grey that stretched up and down the trunk, reaching into the branches. One or two gnarled limbs lifted a little. Twigs untangled.

At the ends of the twigs, tiny green points appeared. They were jammed tight into woody cups with raw red at the base. The green points grew, swelled, opened into sticky spikes.

I looked at Haxforth. He'd stood up now, was moving closer to the tree.

I looked at the sky. The same wintry sheet of cloud we'd had for days.

I raced up the steps of 79 Annandale Avenue and banged on the front door.

Daniel opened it a crack. 'Aidan, you need to go . . .'

'I think you better look at this.'

'What? . . . Oh!'

Daniel stepped down onto the gravelled parking space and stared at the stump and its crown of upraised branches. The green spikes were lengthening, broadening, spreading into dry fleecy-type leaves. Now something else was coming, coming faster, as if inside the tree was picking up speed somehow. Cottonwool white, curling and spinning into life. Blossom. Showers, clouds of white blossom, with rose-coloured hearts and yellow standing heart-hairs.

'But it's been dead *forever* . . .'

I ducked out and glanced up and down the road. There were trees in both directions, neighbours' trees, council trees planted along the kerb, trees in the distance that were part of some allotments. All were bare and dark, motionless in the winter air.

I ran back. A black-and-gold bee hovered among the flowery branches. Already the blossom was shrivelling and coming loose and dropping to the ground. It lay on top of the white fungus, first in scatterings and then in a soft heap like a snowdrift. I wanted to take off my shoes and plunge my feet in but I knew they'd freeze because this was December.

'Dad could never bring himself to cut it down,' Daniel said.

'Sensible man.' Haxforth glanced at us. There was a smile on his face but it was that crooked kind that doesn't really mean happiness.

'What's going on?' I whispered.

But Haxforth didn't answer, only turned back to the tree. It wasn't like you really wanted to talk then anyway, you wanted to watch and nothing else.

With the blossom gone we could see the fruit. Standing up, little orbs on sticks. Quickly they expanded and sagged down in bunches. Green, the colour of emeralds, then reddening as they grew. Apples. And somehow the little tree was bright and its leaves made shadows even though there was no sun in the sky. It was a shady tree, a bursting tree, a tree like you see at midsummer.

A swallow came down, skimming the ground. Round and round it went. On the tree the apples ripened, dropped to the ground. The leaves fell too, turning green-black, then brown, crinkling like chips left too long in the oven. Autumn. Not so long ago. Once more the swallow circled, then we saw its forked tail settle in the branches, saw its body become still and hunch-shouldered.

Two ancient unblinking bird eyes stared at us through the winter-morning gloom.

Haxforth shuddered out a long low breath. With steady hands he approached, with steady hands he plucked the swallow from the tree. He held it like you'd hold a valuable antique. Gently, gently, he folded the wings then tucked the bird inside the front pocket of the foul Admiral hoodie. The apples lay at his feet. There were five or six of them, their surfaces yellowing, softening, the skin rucking up. For a moment or two they looked so yellow they might have been made of gold. But then they were browning too. A wind was stripping the branches. The powdery grey of the bark congealed to black, the death-poison surfacing again. The wind gusted and blew away the fungus and the blossom and the carpet of brown leaves and the shrivelled apples. Soon all of it was gone.

The tree was gnarled and dead. It had been dead for many, many years.

Daniel held the front door open for us. In the metal kitchen we boiled the kettle, made three hot sugary teas.

# 32

We went downstairs to talk. It felt safer. Somehow among the silver machines Mrs Cushway still seemed predatory. Only this time, instead of the outside stairwell with its iron railings, we used the internal connecting door. It was in a corner of the hallway, half hidden by a loaded-up coat stand – the door Daniel'd been so careful to keep locked. Now it was swinging on its hinges.

'The mechanisms can be so complicated these days,' Haxforth said. 'This one was quite straightforward though.'

'You shouldn't have opened it at all,' I told him. 'Don't you know how much trouble you've caused?'

'It practically came apart in my hands.'

'You couldn't open those padlocks in the factory,' Daniel said. 'That one around your ankle, you couldn't get that off.'

'Hard to pick a lock when you've got icicles for fingers.'

Down we went and it was all the same as before – the big

blocky piano, the Great Composers on the wall, the narrow basement window thick with condensation. Haxforth sat on the sofa with its grey geometric shards. There was nothing like the mess Mrs Cushway had said, just a couple of blankets fallen on the floor and some sandwich crusts scattered and a not-so-great smell in the air.

Daniel and I stood in front of him, arms folded.

'What just happened out there? Who are you? We want the *truth* this time.'

'I'm nothing and no-one,' he said, pulling the radiator-style heater in close, switching it on. 'No-one for you to worry about, anyway.'

'Well, how old are you? What does it say on your birth certificate?'

'Birth certificate?' Haxforth looked thoughtful. 'I know what those are. I made a good living for a while, stealing them. Ration cards too. I never had one of my own though. No, not a birth certificate, never one of those.'

'So Aidan's right – you're just a thief?'

'There's more to it than *just*. But yes. It's something I used to be rather good at.'

I grabbed the piano stool, sat down. Haxforth shifted on the ancient-patterned sofa and I stared hard at him, tried to match his mysteriousness with a force and a flex all my own.

'I've watched them all,' he said. 'From the inside of my secret white eye. Peasants, Crusaders, millworkers in their slums. I've met them all and I've stolen from them all. Now, no more.'

He wasn't speaking too loud. We had to hunch in close, to hear his words.

'Crusaders?'

'And their masters. The kings and monsters – Napoleon, Hitler . . .'

'You met *Hitler*?' Daniel said.

'Well, not met, not exactly . . .'

'You can't be such a great thief,' I told him. 'Not if the condition I found you in's anything to go by. If you were really good at it, you'd be driving around in a Rolls-Royce or something.'

'I'm tired. Worn out. I'm so old you can't begin to imagine.'

'OK then, how old *are* you? I mean roughly. You still haven't told us.'

'Roughly? Roughly a thousand years old.'

I laughed out loud. That was insane. But what could you say? Sometimes it's better to let people believe the crazy stuff. He *looked* that old for sure. And then there *had* been the apple tree coming back to life and the swallow returning, so that put the doubt in your mind, made it so you couldn't be completely certain.

'You can't expect us to believe that,' Daniel said.

'I'm not asking you to believe anything.'

'What about the tree?' I said. 'And the bird – why's the bird so important?'

'Old Beautiful?' Haxforth reached into the pocket of the Admiral hoodie. Slowly, carefully, he pulled out the thing that was sheltering inside and held it up for us to see. Outside, moving and flying around, it'd looked fast and agile but now I saw it for what it was, a crusty old bird, unbelievable it should even be alive, with tattered feathers and a face and beak covered in dark pustule-like growths. Worst of all were the eyes, two evil black eyes that stared at you, that if you looked at them too long seemed like they were saying BEWARE.

Instinctively I shifted the piano stool backwards.

'My companion,' Haxforth said, stroking the torn feathers. 'Or my warder, depending on how you look at it. Sometimes he goes away, but always he comes back. A far more frightful creature than Christy, or any of his sort. But finally the time's come for us to part. Isn't that right, eh, Old Beautiful?' He turned the swallow in his hands, brought it up close to his face. When they were almost eye to eye the thing screeched at him, did some weird spitting thing with its beak.

'Doesn't look very happy about it, does he? That's because he knows it's the end for him too. Well, back inside you go then, till tonight.' Haxforth slipped the bird back into the hoodie and cupped his hands around the pocket's openings, cupped it like you see pregnant women do with their baby bumps.

'I don't get it,' Daniel said. 'Why do you need that – thing – before you can go and find your brother?'

'The brother with the voices inside his head . . .' That was what *I* really wanted to hear about of course – not being forced to look at some horrible disgusting old bird.

'Those voices. The first and biggest things I ever stole. That *we* –' Haxforth patted the pocket, correcting himself – 'ever stole. Not that I was given much choice in the matter.'

'You stole them? You mean you took them away?'

'I gave him peace. My brother. Now it's time for me to have a little of my own. That's what the apple tree means. Time to come home, that's what he's saying.'

'He must be very old,' Daniel said.

'No. You're wrong. He's very young. Not much older than you two.'

I didn't say anything. Obviously that was impossible. But

it didn't matter because in that moment I'd made up my mind. Seeing the apple tree blossom and grow fruit like that had clinched it. It had a shape, this plan of mine, and it wasn't vague and right then it was pumping the purest oxygenated blood through the wide healthy chambers of my invincible heart.

'Listen,' I said. 'We'll help you find him. Take you to where he lives, Shuttle Hill.' I glanced at Daniel, saw him nod in agreement. 'We'll try to anyway. Only – well, maybe there's something you can do for me first.'

'Of course,' Haxforth said. 'There's a debt to be paid, I understand that. Without you and those cutters . . .'

'Great. It won't take long. It's going somewhere – a sort of place you visit.'

I saw Daniel shoot me a warning with his eyes. He was a step ahead already.

'When do we leave?' Haxforth asked.

'As soon as we get you tidied up. They won't even let you on the bus, looking like that.'

'There's some old clothes of Dad's upstairs,' Daniel said. 'Some of them might fit.'

They went upstairs, Haxforth taking the thing he called Old Beautiful with him, and I heard the two of them moving around and talking. He must really have left in a hurry, Daniel's dad, I thought – leaving all those history books behind, and clothes too.

After a while of them not coming down I decided to look around the basement room. It was packed full of stuff when you started noticing, not just the big blocky piano. Clear plastic boxes were stacked high on shelves. There was a dead Tamagotchi inside one, and a chew-eared lion and a Pikachu clock without batteries. There were piles of old schoolwork and art projects and things made out of string and toilet rolls. It was like someone had packed away and catalogued the whole of Daniel's childhood. And then there was the table with the pink lamp and the pile of music books, the scores. I picked up a couple and flicked through them. They were mad and impossible, full of dots and squiggles and unpronounceable foreign words. But each sign and symbol corresponded to a note on the piano, I knew that. Could Daniel really make sense of this? And then make music out of it? I looked at the score open on the little shelf above the keyboard. Moonlight Sonata, it said. I reached out a finger, wanting to strike down on a white or a black key, but then I heard someone on the stairs, pulled guiltily away.

'I know where you want to take him, Aidan. I don't think it's such a great idea.'

'Why not? He can help her, I'm sure of it.'

Daniel looked worried. 'Will they even let him in?'

'Don't see why not. It'll probably help. I think the visiting rules say all minors need to be accompanied by an adult. I'll say he's my grandad or something.'

'But what do you expect to happen?'

'How do I know? Maybe nothing. But here's this bloke who's come out of nowhere and who can make something like *that* happen.' I nodded in the direction of the deadened apple tree.

'It looked like he was watching it to me, same as we were.'

'Whatever. It was amazing anyhow.'

'And it only came to life for a couple of minutes before it died again.'

'So?'

'So! So there has to be a rational explanation!'

'Go on, then.'

'I don't know! But just because I don't know it, it doesn't mean there isn't one.'

We lapsed into a bad-tempered silence.

I went up to the piano and plinked a couple of keys. 'You play this a lot then?'

Daniel nodded. '*All* the time. She wants me to go to the Royal Academy in London.'

'Go on, play us something. While we're waiting.'

'What, now?'

'Yeah. He's taking ages.'

Daniel picked up the little stool and sat it back down in front of the piano. 'OK,' he said, a bit reluctant. He did some weird stretching thing with his fingers, and then he started.

I don't suppose I'm too much of an expert. I mean, I know what classical music sounds like because it's something Mum liked to have on every now and then. In fact I had memories of listening to it with her on the radio in our kitchen, back when the kitchen was a warm cosy place and not filled with grease and dirt and unpaid gas bills. She'd sing along with the bits she knew, enjoying herself, and as I watched Daniel playing I suddenly realised *why*. It's because that sort of music is like taking part in a conversation. It's always changing, and you're always part of it, but you don't have to *say* anything. It's a thinking sort of conversation, and that means there's no pressure. Somehow in that no-pressure she'd found a little bit of freedom.

He played on and I thought, Please please this next time I see her let her remember who I am and please let her come home soon and please let everything go back to how it was before.

Daniel did a little rolling flourish and then he stopped and looked up at me. His face was red and I could tell he was embarrassed. 'What do you think?'

'Really good.' I said that because it *had been*.

'Bravo.'

Haxforth stood clapping from the bottom of the stairs. He looked different now, almost like a respectable pensioner. The sports gear was gone and he wore brown pressed trousers and a light blue shirt under an old overcoat. The thin yellow hair was combed across. He'd come down silent as a shadow, without the slightest scuff or misstep, neither of us noticing. There was a bulge in the pocket of the overcoat, so I guessed that was where Old Beautiful was.

They'd let him into Tredegar House dressed like that, no problem.

We bundled up against the cold, counted money. Through the house, down the front steps, past the dead tree. Almost impossible to believe what'd happened to it earlier. For a moment I remembered that doctor on the radio. Mild hallucinations to begin with, auditory and visual.

Thank Christ Daniel had seen it too.

'Not bothering with school today then?' I asked him. He had his keys in his hand, ready to lock up the house behind us.

'No, I don't think so.'

'Not much point, is there, if it's your last week.'

'Not much.'

School. That made me remember something. That and Daniel's piano playing – how he'd made sense of all those dots and squiggles.

'Wait,' I said. 'I wanted to . . .' I ducked back inside quick before he shut the door, ran into the chandelier room, over to the little coffee table thing where I'd left it. Then back outside again.

I opened it at random, the big hardback *Beowulf.* The modern English on one side, the Old English on the other.

I handed it to Haxforth. Slowly he turned the pages.

'What do you think?'

'A beautiful book,' he said. 'Beautiful writing. I've seen them before – these shapes, you understand.'

He pointed at the weird angular runes.

I looked at Daniel. 'Where?' I said. 'Where have you seen them?'

'A man I met once. He could read these words. Could write them too.'

'But nobody writes like that,' Daniel said. 'It's nowhere near proper English. It's not even the right alphabet.'

Haxforth shrugged. 'All the same. He showed me how. All his writing equipment ranged out, I remember. We shared a room once at an inn. Wore a black priest's cloak.' Haxforth moved his fingers over the grainy pages of the book. 'An inquisitive sort, hardly religious at all. Discovered I was a thief somehow, and after that he wouldn't leave me alone. Wanted to know all about it.'

'What did you tell him?'

'Ah. Well. Stories, that was what he was really after. Kept saying I must know *one or two*, on account of my travels and profession.'

'And did you? Know any, I mean?'

'Of course.' Haxforth smiled. 'The old ones, naturally – the ones I'd heard as a child. He hurried me through those though, said he'd heard them all before. A very provoking fellow, he was. Full of noise and sly flattery. Impossible to escape from. After a while I found myself sugaring the pill.'

'Sugaring the pill?'

'Thief's prerogative. He wanted tales, so that's what I gave him. Gold excited him particularly. And dragons. He was convinced *those* were real. I simply . . . helped him along. What else did he expect? He plied me with ale till dawn. A thoroughly provoking fellow. Curious, that I remember him so well.'

'Have a read,' I said. 'Tell me if you recognise any of it.'

Haxforth looked at me, embarrassed. 'I can't.'

'He means the modern English, not the old stuff,' Daniel told him.

'I can't read that either.'

'You can't *read*?' said Daniel. '*At all?*'

'Short words sometimes. Signs, things like that. Otherwise . . . No.'

I took the book out of his hands, stuck it back inside the house. We could stand there forever puzzling out the past, but how clever was it really when there was the small matter of the future to think of?

'Let's go,' I said.

We walked out under sheet-metal skies, heading for the nearest bus stop.

# 33

A smooth connection to the high street, scanning the dense-packed shoppers for Christy or any of his pals. Everything was Peace and Goodwill. Haxforth didn't seem rattled by the crowds and the crowds took no notice of him, had their heads stuffed with a million other things. We weaved between them invisible. The time on the bus-stop board said 10.02. A few minutes' wait for the right one and then we climbed to the top deck where you always go even when it's empty downstairs. Off it lurched, moving up the gears, a brightly lit box travelling through a dark winter's morning.

'I'm pretty sure this'll take us right by it,' I said. 'Tredegar House – there's a big sign and a car park. Press the button if you see it.'

'I can't see anything out of these windows.' Daniel wiped at the misted-up glass with his coat sleeve.

I leaned forward, hung my arms over the headrest of the

seat in front where Haxforth was sitting. I was in a sprawling-out sort of mood, happy and wanting to talk. *Control.* That was what it was all about. That was the whole game. The ability to change direction, to decide where you're going and then to get there. Control was what I'd been lacking all this time. I'd played catch-up too long, forgotten what it meant to streak ahead.

Haxforth and Mum. Yes. The idea was getting stronger by the minute. You hold a rag into the wind, you want to see if it flies or falls to the ground. What did the doctors at Tredegar House know anyway? I'd heard Dad say it himself once: I don't think even they know what they're doing up there half the time.

All those drugs they were giving her, turning her into a zombie – it wasn't working. I mean, doctors can't know everything there is to know in this world, can they?

And what was the worst that could happen? Even if I was kidding myself about this whole thing? I'd sit and talk to Mum and say all the things I really wanted her to hear but couldn't say last time. Maybe just doing that and holding her hand at the same time would help, in some small way.

I tapped Haxforth on the shoulder but only got a grunt in response. I leaned forward and saw his eyes were closed. Probably having a nap. It was warm enough up there that that would be a nice thing to do. Most of the other passengers' heads were lolling like the oxygen was running out. I leaned back and moved my fingers across the window-glass, making trickles in the condensation. Tried to relax a bit. I listened to the engine and watched the streets and the people fly by outside. Daniel, across the aisle, was doing the same.

I wondered what Dad was doing. Was he out there somewhere in his Royal Mail uniform, working his round?

I knew he wasn't.

Would he even be around tonight, when I went home?

Then a freaky thing happened. Really freaky. I *saw* him. The bus was shooting by the Turkish supermarket and past the little street that leads off from there and as I looked down it *I saw him.* He was arguing with that other postie guy, Hawkie. Or rather, Hawkie was arguing with him. You could tell that from the wide aggressive way he was standing, hand and finger stabbing the air.

Gone already. But no doubt it was him.

I moved a few seats forward, banged open a window, let cold air pour across my face. The memory of the mail came lunging back, the images of it piled in the shed, getting higher and higher by the day. Somehow, with everything else that'd happened that morning, I'd managed to forget about it for a while. Now it came in, full force. That's the worst thing about really bad stuff, when it happens in your life. You think about it all the time anyway but when you *do* stop, just for a minute or two, suddenly it surges at you brimmed-up with heart-clutching power. All those people not getting their mail. Not just the Christmas presents but the really important stuff, like Annie Fraser-Howe's letter.

Hawkie and Dad arguing like that. What could it mean? Information? Threat? Warning?

I made a decision then – another one.

I'd do it, the thing I should've done right at the start if only I hadn't been so scared because of everything that was happening with Mum. I couldn't deal with it any more, not with Christmas coming. So I'd confront him, I'd tell Dad what I'd been doing. Prise open those Lines of Communication. Let him know what was coming down the track. Maybe, secretly, that was even what he was waiting for. Then we could work on clearing it together, if it wasn't too late.

Yes. First Mum. Then get Haxforth off to where he'd be looked after. Then confront Dad.

That was it, my whole entire plan.

Today *everything* was going to change.

# 34

We didn't have to worry about missing the stop. It came up anyway on the automatic announcer. Another group, from down below, got off with us. Some of them began to walk in the direction of Tredegar House. I'd never thought about that before, how the other people in there with Mum had brothers and sisters and sons and daughters and friends too.

'Must be the start of visiting hours,' I said. 'We timed it just right.'

Daniel grabbed me by the elbow. 'Are you sure about this?'

'Sure I'm sure.'

'But what if he, I don't know, freaks her out or something? He's pretty weird, isn't he? I really think you should leave things like this to the doctors.'

I stopped, turned. Waited for Haxforth. He'd fallen behind a bit. What harm could a doddering old man possibly do?

Daniel was being too cautious. His whole *personality* was too cautious. Somebody needed to tell him that sometime.

As soon as we got inside we saw that a couple of people from the bus had stopped at the empty enquiries office, were pressing the bell for attention. We shot past, headed straight for the waiting lift. I still hadn't told Haxforth where we were or why I'd brought him here and now inside the lift there was a nurse or someone official like that so I couldn't talk to him there either. What the hell, I thought, maybe it's better if all this is spontaneous. Whatever *all this* is.

The nurse inched away from Haxforth as the lift went up. Some of that rank smell was still clinging despite the change of clothes. And then old people have that particular smell anyway, don't they, like dirt or old newspaper print's been welded right down into their wrinkled overscrubbed seams. You'd've thought a nurse would be used to that though.

At the fourth floor we got off and there was a bench right opposite the lifts and Daniel said he was going to wait there because he really didn't know about this, didn't want to go any further.

'That's fine,' I said. 'You can look after Haxforth's coat for us while we're gone.'

I hadn't forgotten the ancient pustule-covered swallow stowed inside the overcoat's pocket. It didn't seem such a great idea, taking something like that past the airlock doors and into Mum's room.

Daniel put his hands up, shook his head. A reflex reaction and I knew why. Nobody'd want to go near that repulsive thing unless they had to. Nobody that is except Haxforth. Hearing my suggestion he'd pulled the coat tight around him, not wanting to take it off or part with it so that I stood there a moment uncertain, trying to decide how important this really was while being super-aware all the time that we weren't exactly even supposed to be there in the first place.

'Those pockets have got zips,' Daniel said. 'Nothing's getting out of them.'

'Let's see.' I was reaching out a hand to check, because although the overcoat was well padded it still looked kind of frayed, when the lift doors opened again and out stepped another nurse.

'You're Mary Hale's son, aren't you?' she said, catching my eye. 'I remember you. Your father was here till late last night.'

'Oh,' I said. 'Was he?' That drove a spike of numbness down inside. Why couldn't he include me? And what happened afterwards, for him not to come home?

The nurse glanced at Haxforth but there wasn't anything like suspicion in the look. 'It's nice you've found somebody else to bring you. Give him a break. Who's this – your granddad?'

'Yeah. My granddad.' I looked her right in the eye as I said it, kept everything blank and neutral. Your face is your mask, your protection, it's not a set of traffic lights.

'In you come, then.'

I shrugged at Daniel, told him we'd see him in a while, that we'd only be up the corridor, and then I beckoned to Haxforth and together we followed the nurse along to the buzzer by the door with the oblong of reinforced glass. It was just like before, the card-swipe through the entry point, the Harley-Davidson man standing chewing a mouthful of T-shirt, the leather sofas smelling like public toilets, the nurses all wearing those plastic aprons.

'Come on, I'll take you to her room,' the nurse told us. 'Then my shift really *is* over. Home to a hot bath and a cup of cocoa.' She winked at Haxforth. 'Or something stronger.'

We went along the corridor, Harley-Davidson man ambling after us like he did last time.

'What is this place, Aidan?' Haxforth whispered.

No time to answer though. Corridor's end already, the door to Mum's room.

'Great news, isn't it?' said the nurse.

'What news?'

'About your mum going home tomorrow.'

I just froze, hearing that. It was like all my muscles went into lockdown or something. Maybe I'd heard wrong? But the smile on the nurse's face told me No, she'd said it and meant it all right.

Haxforth stared at me and I knew then that he'd made the connection: Mary Hale who hears voices like your brother did once and do you think you can do anything to help her like you must have done with him? He wasn't exactly looking overjoyed about it either.

Haxforth with those eyes that looked like the back of his skull was showing through. Haxforth who'd told us that he'd been around for a thousand years. Wild and emaciated and rotten-mouthed he struck me as now, beside this neat plump nurse. *And* with that thing stuffed into his overcoat pocket. All the certainty I'd felt earlier, after seeing the apple tree blossom, drained away right then. It was gone in about a tenth of a second. You would not believe it, how fast a thing like that can die.

I was taking this person into a room to meet *Mum*? Someone who spent her time hiding from or battling against those things that tormented her, but still breathing after all – not only breathing, but improving. *Going home.*

'There she is,' said the nurse, holding the door open for us. 'Some people to see you, Mrs Hale. Well, aren't you going in?'

# 35

'Hello, Mum.'

'Hello, Aidan.'

'Are you feeling better?'

'I – I think so.'

She was sitting up in bed, propped by pillows, still white and swollen in her nightgown like her arms and legs had melted into the rest of her body. I went towards her, wanting to hold her, wanting her to hold me, but then I saw deep in the sleepy eyes a glimpse of that old look, the look of confusion and alarm, the wanting to get away, so I just sat on the end of the bed and felt the weight of her foot against my side.

She knows my name, I thought. That's good. That's really good.

'Came to see you,' I said.

From the corner of my eye I saw the nurse leave the room. Haxforth was already sitting in the one single chair. He'd moved it right away from the bed. His eyes, what I could see of them, were puckered and near-focused, like a weightlifter's when he's about to snatch the bar. His arms were fixed and folded across his middle. The bird in the zippered coat pocket seemed to be moving around under them quite a bit.

'They told me you're coming home. That's so great. We'll get you all comfortable and you won't have to go out, not at all if you don't want to.'

'I can't wait,' said Mum. 'I hate this place. It's full of nutters, crazy people.'

'Yeah,' I said. 'Are you taking all the medicines they're giving you?'

'I'm taking everything. Handfuls of pills. It's all I ever do.'

It was funny, all the drugs they'd been prescribing had made her put on weight, turned her skin to hard yellow wax, made her look more solid than she ever did before. But somehow it felt like the real her, the real Mum, was flickering inside, buried deep, a candle flame that might go out with the slightest breath.

She nudged her foot against my side. 'Who's that? Do I know him?'

'That's Haxforth. He's sort of a friend of mine.'

'He's a ghost,' Mum said.

I tried to smile, tried to look at Haxforth – still refusing eye contact.

'I mean it. He's a ghost.'

'He's not a ghost, Mum. He's just someone I know.'

'I'm telling you, he's a—'

But Mum didn't finish what she was saying because all of a sudden Haxforth was standing up, standing and waving his hands in the air. He was saying something too with his mouth wide open but I couldn't understand what and I couldn't look at him anyway to try to understand better because by then I'd seen how Old Beautiful, its two eyes like black thorns somehow, had escaped from the overcoat and was loose in the room.

Mum, when I looked back at her, was whimpering. I knew straightaway from her eyes how scared she was. It was like a fear-supernova exploding inside there.

Oh god oh Jesus.

'Catch him!' shouted Haxforth. But I didn't even try. Old Beautiful was going too fast, making jagged runs in the air, hitting walls. It left a smear as it collided with the window in the door. I saw the blue of the body and the red at its throat, it was crazy possessed, feathers beak and claws everywhere. Haxforth moved after it with his skinny old man's arms, hands snapping together to grasp but always a split second too late. *I* was more worried about protecting Mum. She hadn't moved a muscle, hadn't even pulled the bedsheets over her head like maybe another frightened person would've done. Perhaps she saw things like this all the time, I don't know. Perhaps she fought every day to stop them coming through from her shadow mind and now here was one breaking through for real.

This next bit, I can hardly bring myself to write down.

Somehow Old Beautiful banged against or got through the hands that I had out protecting encircling Mum. Its claws skimmed the topmost part of her neglected hair and snagged and then next thing the whole bird was tangled up there and I heard its tiny scream and saw the wings beating right in her face so it almost looked like it was trying to attack her and there was some blood already from her scalp. I thrust my fists in there, right into the screaming thrashing mess that was Mum's head, and Haxforth was doing the same and somehow I don't know how we got it disentangled and when we lifted it away there were feathers in Mum's hair so she looked like some mad Indian goddess, only she wasn't acting too much like a goddess what with all the screaming she was doing by then.

The door burst open and a nurse came running in, not the nurse from before. I don't know what she was expecting but right away she took a step back seeing the bird, locked in Haxforth's hands now like a seed in a seedpod. The same reaction as Daniel and understandable really because it looked like some plague-carrying thing you'd only ever see in a nightmare. Just glancing at it made you feel sick to your stomach.

She looked from me to Mum and from Mum to Haxforth and Old Beautiful. She saw the feathers in Mum's hair, the blood on her scalp where the claws'd cut.

'Where did it come from?' She stared at me. 'Did *you* bring it in?' They hadn't taught her to deal with anything like this at nursing school, you could tell that by the shock in her voice.

I didn't give her an answer. I couldn't. I looked at the floor, wanted to burrow right down into it with my eyes and never have to come out above the surface again.

'She was meant to be going home tomorrow. The doctors thought she'd levelled out. What have you *done* to her?'

'I – I'm sorry . . .'

Mum was just staring at her hands laid in her lap. The screaming was over. Her eyes were glassy. There didn't seem to be any light behind them any more. That's it, I thought. The flickering-inside candle's gone out. I killed it.

'What will your father say? You *are* her son, aren't you?'

I nodded.

The nurse held the door open. She didn't say anything else. She didn't have to.

'I love you, Mum,' I said, my voice trembling. 'I've got to go now. You'll feel better soon.'

I felt useless saying that. But I had to say something. I pulled the door shut behind me, leaving the nurse inside with Mum.

I walked along the corridor. Behind me I heard other nurses being called into Mum's room. One of them was running. I waited by the main door until someone let me out. Haxforth was next to me, not that I really cared too much about him at that moment. Daniel was still waiting on the bench. He opened his mouth to say something but then he saw the expression on my face and thought better of it.

I got into the lift. I hardly knew which button to press, I felt so dead and numb and kicked about inside.

We walked down the driveway of Tredegar House and waited at the bus stop in silence.

'What do we do now?' Daniel asked after a little while.

I turned away. I didn't feel so much like talking to him or anyone else just then. My throat was all closed up and my eyes were prickly and damp. What I was thinking it'd be really good to do was walk a bit further along, to where there was a bend in the road. The buses came along there nice and fast. When the next one zipped by, I'd throw myself right under it.

# 36

I didn't do that though. A bus pulled in but all I did was get on it. It was heading back into town. The journey took five hours, five minutes, five seconds – how should I know? Daniel and Haxforth talking in the seats behind, the cars and roads and verges, the Christmas-busy high street, all of it swished past. My head was too busy exploding with what'd just happened. Why hadn't Dad *told* me she was coming home? Did he want to surprise me or something? But then how could he tell me anything when I hadn't seen him for ages – not to talk to at least. Where was he? And what was he going to say, when he found out about this? Because there was no doubting that he would. The very next time he went up there, to Tredegar House, they'd let him in on the whole story. Your son and some old man, some strange-looking type, and this bird they brought into her room, that attacked her . . .

Oh Christ. And there'd been me all set on confronting him

about the mail, thinking maybe we could get it delivered together and then enter into some Bright New Era of father-son relations.

Daniel tapped me on the shoulder and the three of us were standing again on concrete pavements, watching the bus drive away.

'I thought this was the best place to get off,' he said. 'Close to your house.'

Great. Maresfield Crescent was only a couple of streets away, coming from this direction. Pretty much the last place on earth I wanted to go. My own fault though, for not paying attention.

'Look, show him,' Daniel said to Haxforth, pulling at the old overcoat. Haxforth opened up the front and pointed a finger. There was a hole in the lining of the pocket there, and that was how Old Beautiful had got out.

'It wasn't your fault, that's the point.' From the way Daniel said it I knew Haxforth must've clued him in. There wasn't any *I told you so* though. He could easily have done that. It would've paid me back for all those times I'd bullied him to get dinner money. Daniel just wasn't the type. He was a good person to have on your side. I wished I'd seen it earlier.

'The hole wasn't that big before,' Haxforth muttered. 'It was careless of me.'

'Careless!' I could've stamped and shouted at that. Once, I would've done. But I knew it wasn't right to blame Haxforth – him or his weird possessed bird. No, there was only one person to blame, only one person who'd insisted we go to Tredegar House. That was the one person I'd never be able to get away from.

'Where is it now?' I asked.

'In the other pocket.'

'Oh, that's fantastic. That's really excellent.'

'Why's it so special?' Daniel said. 'You never told us, not really. Why do you call it – him – Old Beautiful?'

Haxforth wrapped the coat tighter, laid one protective hand on the new place where the swallow lay resting or sleeping, or at least that was what I supposed it was doing since there was no movement there now. 'Why? Because Old Beautiful was made by Old Magic. As was I. Both of us kept alive a thousand years, so a kingdom might prosper.'

'Old Magic!' Daniel said.

'You're right to laugh. It doesn't exist any more. But it did once, when things like this were made.'

Haxforth opened the white palm of his other hand. A gold clasp lay there – a coiled hinge at one end and an arrowhead catch at the other. Even in the dishwater daylight it glittered like sunshine.

Daniel's hand flew down to his jeans pocket, tore out the matchbox he had in there, opened it.

'You took it!' he said. 'Right out of my pocket!'

'*And* put back the matchbox.'

'But these pockets are really tight! How did you . . . ?'

'On the bus,' Haxforth said. 'It was easy.'

He held the clasp out in my direction, but I motioned for him to give it straight back to Daniel. I wasn't about to forget that promise I'd made. Daniel put it back inside the little cardboard box, dug it all down deeper than ever into his jeans.

'We'll help you to get to Shuttle Hill,' I said. 'Right now. We'll buy some food on the way. Won't we, Daniel?'

Daniel nodded. 'If it's as near as you say, we can probably be back by tonight.'

I was tired of everything, that was the truth. So, so tired.

It'd been weeks since I slept properly. I'd just made the worst decision of my entire life. The consequences'd be off the scale. Whatever the truth about Haxforth, I wanted to get lost in it for a while, get swept along, not have to think any more about *being me*.

The only thing is, it doesn't really work, forgetting about yourself or your situation, when the world insists on sending out reminders.

We were crossing the road, the three of us, about to start for Shuttle Hill wherever exactly it might be, when a red Royal Mail van shot through the junction of the next road along. Even when he was doing his job like he was paid to, Dad was on deliveries, not collections, and he never had a van. So this couldn't be him. But something about the way it was being driven set off alarm bells and then watching it turn left I knew for sure, because of the one-way signs they have around there. Instantly the pictures were playing in my head, bright like on a screen at the multiplex: Dad's mountain of stolen post, that I'd worked so hard to deliver and keep secret, getting dragged into the open, and all the important men in wigs and uniforms staring and glaring and saying their piece and then soon after jail for Dad and care home for me and permanent hospital maybe for Mum, since there wouldn't be anyone else to look after her.

Stuff like that you can't run away from, even if you are standing next to a bloke who says he's been kept alive for a thousand years by *Old Magic*.

# 37

'Do you want me to come with you?'

Daniel'd seen the Royal Mail van too and knew what it meant. Or at least he knew it meant trouble – big immediate trouble.

I shook my head. Somebody had to keep an eye on Haxforth. 'I'll be back just as soon as . . .'

Daniel nodded. He got the picture. I didn't have to explain anything to him.

Through the familiar streets at a run, hitting Maresfield Crescent fast. Breath like a steam pump and the clouds dark and drooping above so it felt like evening already, one of those winter days that's over before it begins.

There. My house. The red Royal Mail van parked plum outside and the clicking closing gate wide off its latch for once.

I felt sick, my stomach twisting inside out.

Right away I knew what was happening. There wasn't

anybody inside the house. It was dark and closed up like when I'd left it. I hadn't really been expecting that anyway.

The garden. The shed. The door that didn't even have a lock, standing open now.

Mail hurled out over the grass.

And somebody inside, thrashing around and swearing.

I went nearer. I couldn't hide any more or pretend this wasn't happening.

A figure appeared in the doorway. It was wearing Royal Mail boots and a Royal Mail coat. Shorts even though it was December. Big black tattoos on both legs. A red Santa hat on its head.

'Keep your mouth shut,' Hawkie growled.

He turned back inside the shed and I went over to the door to watch him.

'I don't see why little kids should suffer just cause your dad can't be arsed to do his job any more.' Hawkie was shoving all the Christmas presents he could find into grey mail sacks. It was obvious which ones they were – anything wrapped in brown paper, oddly shaped, plastered with bright stamps. There were quite a few. They didn't weigh much though, and Hawkie seemed to have plenty of sacks. They were all almost full already. I took out my torch and switched it on, shone it into the darker corners.

'Bloody waste of space, he is,' Hawkie said. He gathered up fistfuls of sacks and barged past me. He could carry a *lot*. He took them down the passageway, out through the gate, and I heard the metal doors of the van open and the sacks going in. The ones left over I picked up, wanting to help, but he was back already intercepting me in the passageway.

He snatched them out of my hand. The torch got snatched

too but he didn't seem to notice that. You could see he was mad and furious as hell.

'Do you know how much fucking shit he's caused me?' he said. 'Do you know how long I've been trying to cover for him?'

'I'm sorry, I'm really sorry.'

Hawkie said some more swear words about Dad and then he turned to go.

'Can I have my torch back?' I said.

'What?'

'My torch – can I have it back?'

Hawkie looked at his fist, at the clutch of bags there and the torch in among them. 'Oh yeah,' he said. 'Here you go.'

'Thanks.'

He sort of paused then and looked at me almost like he was seeing me for the first time. 'How old are you now, Aidan? Thirteen? Fourteen?'

'Fourteen,' I said. 'And a half.'

'You poor bastard.'

He didn't say it nasty or mean but in a sad sort of way, like he really meant it. That didn't make me feel so great. He put the bags down.

'If you see your dad, tell him this. But you never heard it from me, right? Seven o'clock tomorrow morning, you're going to be getting a little visit. Two of the top guys from Royal Mail, investigators. They're bringing the police with them. Right here.'

'How do you know that?' I breathed.

'It doesn't matter how I know. And you didn't hear it from me, OK?'

'OK.'

'Aidan, they're coming for the mail and they're going to arrest your dad, do you understand me?'

'I understand,' I whispered.

'I tried my best, but with some people . . .' Hawkie picked up the fistful of bags. 'Well, there's no rest for Santa's little elves, is there?'

'No,' I said.

He reached out his free hand and shook mine. 'Good luck, mate.'

He carried the bags out through the gate, put them in the back of the Royal Mail van, and sped away.

# 38

I stood there in the darkening passageway with only torchlight for company and it was like the sick feeling, the twisting inside-out feeling, had exploded up into my chest. For a moment I thought it might even shut down the invincible heart for good. All the mail I'd delivered. The mail Daniel had delivered. It meant nothing now, precisely nothing. A total waste. I limped over to the square of grass at the back of our house and scooped up a few handfuls of mail, flung them inside the shed. But then I stopped because what was the point? My arms and legs didn't seem to be working properly anyway, they felt heavy and misshapen somehow, dragging, dragging.

Now, finally, it was going to happen. The knock on the door I'd been dreading all that time.

Focus, focus, try to think of a plan. Or anything at all, anything positive.

*Good luck.* Why had Hawkie said that? In fact, why had he warned me *at all*?

So I could do something about it.

What if there was some way of making the post disappear, before tomorrow morning? That way there'd be NO EVIDENCE. I thought about burning it, making a bonfire in the garden, feeding the mail into the flames until all of it was gone forever. But no, that wouldn't work. It'd take hours and some of it might not burn at all. Besides, the neighbours would see and get curious. And then, even if I *could* burn everything, there'd still be the mountains of ash to get rid of and the scorch marks on the lawn to explain.

What about dumping it, in some wood somewhere, or at the bottom of a river? But no, that wouldn't work either. The only woods I knew were full of dog-walkers, and a river – well, how would I make it sink? Even if I bagged up the mail securely enough, it would take more than a few stones to weigh it all down. It would take whole *paving slabs*. Lots of them. Where was I going to get those from? And how would I move them? On the rusting racer? No chance.

And anyway, even supposing I *could* do all that, there was mail in there – mail at my feet – that mattered. It wasn't *all* broadband offers and holiday brochures. What about the other Annie Fraser-Howes out there, waiting for the things they really really needed?

No. Getting rid of it – even if it was practical, I couldn't do anything like that.

*Good luck.*

Maybe if Dad handed himself in, owned up before they came for him, he could avoid jail somehow. Avoid a custodial sentence. That happens sometimes, doesn't it?

No. Fourteen months that man in Birmingham, Matthew Greenwood, got for doing the exact same thing.

*We will always prosecute anybody who abuses their position of trust in our organisation.*

What then? *Good luck*. It was almost like Hawkie was trying to give me a head start.

Then I knew.

I fished my house key out of my pocket and went inside. It felt like stepping into a giant refrigerator. I turned on the lights, looked at the red bill from the gas company still tucked under the fruit bowl, at the shrivelled apple, brown and rotten and starting to liquefy, at the cold coagulating swamp in the kitchen sink. The place smelled disgusting, like the bins at the back of school before they get emptied.

The clock on the microwave said 15.11.

Move fast now and no hanging around.

I raced upstairs, gathered jeans and jumpers, anything thick I could find, stuffed them into a bag, found a pair of shoes that were the nearest things I had to boots and laced them tight. Collected up my toothbrush and deodorant, dropped those in the bag too. What else, what else? There had to be other things, other things I'd need through these coldest nights of the year.

'Aidan?' I heard someone call. 'Aidan?'

I glanced out of a window, saw two figures standing uncertainly on the front path. Daniel and Haxforth. I ran down, showed them into the lounge. The dusty shelves, the dictionary, the sofa where Dad watched Premier League. Curtains closed, closed all winter. It could all go to hell now.

'We waited but you didn't come . . .' Daniel said. 'I saw the van drive away.'

'Don't get comfortable,' I said. 'We're not stopping.'

I told him about Hawkie and what he'd told me.

'You're kidding,' Daniel whispered. 'You don't mean you're really going to . . . ?'

Yes, I thought. I really do mean that. They can't take me into care if they can't find me. There's nothing for me here any more. So what I'll do is, I'll go with Haxforth, help him find his brother, see if there's anything for me there. That'd be a nice thing to do, a helpful and positive thing, and maybe from doing that one good and positive thing other good and positive things would follow, like people are always telling you they do. But even if nothing like that happened, I still wouldn't turn back. I'd go on somewhere else. Haxforth had done it, hadn't he? He'd gone from place to place, owning nothing, knowing nothing, only how to steal and survive. And he'd lived long enough.

Anyway, I was leaving Maresfield Crescent forever, right now, and that was final.

I went over to the mantelpiece, to the wedding picture in its frame. Taking it out, wanting a keepsake, I saw something else tucked beneath, another photo. Us as a family in the sun. Eating ice creams, sitting on a beach, I didn't know where. Dad brown and bare-chested, me wearing a superhero T-shirt, still a little kid. Mum smiling. Just smiling. No confusion in her eyes. I'd never seen her look so happy and uncomplicated. Best picture ever. Why hadn't I seen this before?

I put it carefully inside the flattest part of my leaving-home bag.

'Come on,' I said, opening the front door. 'We're going.'

Daniel rubbed his hands warm and adjusted the zip on his coat but Haxforth, perched on the brown sofa, stayed where he was. 'Do you have any water?' he said. 'It's not for me, it's for Old Beautiful.'

Oh Christ, I thought. He'd taken the swallow out of the overcoat pocket, was holding it like one of those doves they release at Olympic ceremonies and other things like that, only it looked more like a bird of World Disease than World Peace.

'Quickly then,' I said. 'Just don't let go of it, whatever you do.'

'Don't worry. I won't let him fly until we reach Shuttle Hill.'

I ran into the kitchen for a bowl of water, feeling desperate, wanting to get out, wanting to put miles between me and Maresfield Crescent, but then I saw an old plastic lunchbox up on a shelf, a big deep thing with a clip-down lid, so I grabbed that too and stabbed some holes in it with one of the sharp knives we'd hidden from Mum, thinking it'd be a more secure place to keep Old Beautiful than a frayed overcoat pocket. Back in the lounge Daniel was asking Haxforth how far, exactly, this Shuttle Hill place was.

'Oh . . . a few miles . . .'

'How many though?'

Haxforth shrugged. I gave him the water and the plastic lunchbox, showed him how the clips worked. Old Beautiful's head bobbed out from between his two clutching hands, drinking and bathing its pustuled face.

'Well, how are we going to get there? Bus, or—'

'Walk.'

'*Walk?*' said Daniel. 'In this cold? Are you mad? Anyway, it'll be pitch black in a couple of hours. As soon as we leave town we won't be able to see a thing.'

'Full moon,' Haxforth said. 'High around midnight.' His

eyes looked at us like moons themselves – those eyes that seemed to say everything and nothing all at the same time.

'But it'll take all night . . .'

'I'm going,' I said. '*I'll* walk it. Come on, Daniel.' I shot him a look. I knew he was thinking about his mum, about what'd happen if he wasn't home by the time she got back from her day in court. I knew too that he didn't want to mention any of that because of *my* situation. 'Look, can't we debate this outside? Anywhere except here?'

Too late. Out on the Crescent I heard a car doing a quick sloppy parking manoeuvre. A door slammed. Footsteps blasted through the clicking closing gate. Dad stood Satan-faced in the passageway.

It knew what'd happened at Tredegar House, this nightmare face.

It said, forget about opening up any Lines of Communication.

Go straight to Apocalypse Now.

# 39

I tried to get the door shut but already he had a foot wedged inside, was trying at the same time to grab me. The best and only thing to do was get out of the way. I turned, tried to turn and make it into the kitchen where at least I could get the table between us if things got too bad but somehow he had me pinned and twisting back by the arm.

'Dad, you're hurting me . . .'

'You stupid – you piece of—'

'Dad!'

He shoved me hard then and the arm of my coat rode up as I put my hands out to stop the fall and some part of me grazed the edge of the kitchen door and there was a smear of blood left on the woodwork but it wasn't too bad. Half running half crawling I made it into the kitchen and around the protecting bulk of the table. Dad was right behind me and snatching. He hadn't even glanced into the lounge, hadn't seen

Daniel or Haxforth. Christ only knew what'd happen when he did.

'Where have you been?' I shouted, hoping that'd distract him somehow.

'Never you mind! I've just come from there and the nurses told me everything.'

'I wanted to see her. You never take me – only that one time – so I went on my own!'

'It wasn't you on your own though, was it? There was some other bloke with you, some old bloke. That's what they told me. And he had some bird thing that attacked her . . . What was it Aidan, some sick game? Some weird kind of bet?'

His breath was really fast and jaggedy and he grabbed at me again but missed this time.

'I wanted to see her, I wanted to help . . .'

'Wanted to *help*? Do you know how upset she was after that visit? One of the male nurses had to restrain her, did you know that?'

My throat tightened. I tried to swallow, couldn't. Oh god oh Jesus. There was a pricking round my eyes, tears threatening again. I couldn't explain, how could I tell him about the dead apple tree and how it came back to life, and all the things Haxforth had said about people who hear voices inside their heads? How could I, when I didn't even understand it myself?

I didn't move and neither did he. The kitchen table between us. He looked a state. There were thick black rings around his eyes despite all the sleeping tablets, his chin was unshaved, his trousers were flecked with dried mud below the knees.

'You know the deal with those places?' he said. 'What nobody tells you? Once you're in there you have to get out fast, before it becomes the only place you can handle. There's people – years they've been in there. It's like some nightmare conveyor belt, once you're on you can't get off. And they were *going to let her out.* She was doing OK, on some new drugs that seemed to be helping, but now you've gone and sent her mental again and god knows what'll happen . . .'

I didn't speak. My face was starting to feel pretty wet and snot-mangled.

'Stop snivelling,' Dad said, and that was OK, I didn't mind him telling me that because it meant he might be calming down a bit. But then he did the worst thing he could possibly've done. He turned around and glanced into the lounge and saw Daniel and Haxforth sitting there, side by side now on the brown sofa with the closed plastic lunchbox between them.

For a moment it was like he was too stunned to move. He couldn't believe what his eyes were telling him. Then he tore off his coat and stepped straight-backed towards Haxforth, the menace level turned up full and extreme.

'Is this *him?* Is this the bloke with the bird, who you took to see Mum?'

'Dad . . .'

'I don't believe this.'

His clenched fists were the colour of snow.

I darted under the table and ran between Haxforth and the advancing figure of Dad. I knew he was going to snap Haxforth in half or at least try to and I couldn't bear that. It didn't matter if Dad hit me but if he hit Haxforth then he'd be no better than Christy, and I knew he was, deep down I knew he was, even if he hadn't shown it for a while.

'And who the fuck's this little toerag? What the *hell's* been going on here?'

Daniel was trying to make himself as small as possible and

I thought, Here you go, Daniel, this is what it's like to have your father around, they're not all wonderful you know.

Violence hung in the air, a gaping dragon-mouth ready to shred and annihilate. It was seconds away and I knew then that I had to do something to push this Dad away and bring back the real one, the Dad from before, and I had to do it right there and then because he was about to cross over into some other place, some permanent place that'd only ever be filled with shadow and anger.

It was what I should've done right at the start of all this.

I slammed through the front door, leaving it wide and open to the winter's afternoon, ran down the passageway and into the garden where the light was going already and I scooped up an armful of mail and I ran back inside and threw it right at Dad's face.

And I said, as Haxforth himself had said to me once, 'You want to know what's going on? *That's* what's going on.'

Then I ran outside again and grabbed another concertina of mail and I threw that in his face too, all the red rubber bands and the bright Christmas stamps and I did it again and again and he wasn't stopping me and I was super-shaky and trembling and in the dusk I saw some blood which'd dripped down from the graze on my arm but it didn't hurt or anything.

Dimly I was aware of the people inside the house swapping places. Now Daniel and Haxforth were standing, backed against a wall, and it was Dad sitting slumped on the brown sofa. Funny, I was shouting something too that whole time but I've no idea what. I'd always thought it'd be Dad going crazy when the secret came out. Instead he was the silent one and it was me screaming my head off.

I stopped when the floor of the lounge was covered because by then I'd made my point.

'I was going to deliver it,' Dad said quietly.

'No, you weren't. *I've* been delivering it. And him, he's helped.' I pointed at Daniel. 'Not any more though.'

Then I said about Hawkie, and the cops and the Royal Mail investigators who'd be arriving at seven o'clock tomorrow morning, and how they were going to arrest him.

Dad put his head in his hands. All the aggression was gone. It was just knocked clean away. I saw him take in the bag I'd packed, notice for the first time how thickly I was wrapped against the winter. His face'd gone as white as a fridge-front. I never saw anyone change as fast as that. It was like all the air inside'd been sucked out. His eyes went down to the floor and his hands shifted a little to cover them over.

I kicked a shower of post towards him. 'Where have you even *been*?'

'Just around,' he mumbled. 'In the car. Driving places.'

'All night?'

Only silence, for an answer. I supposed that meant yes.

'How could she come home anyway with all this here?'

'I don't know, Aidan. I don't know. She couldn't. That's what I was trying to work out. If there's any way, any way at all, out of this . . . mess.'

The way he held his bent-over head though told me he hadn't come up with anything during that whole night he'd been away. Not one single solution.

Daniel was crouching down in a corner of the room, staring at the white and brown heaps. 'If we sorted through it,' he said slowly, like he was trying to persuade himself, 'took out the really important things and made sure they were delivered, wouldn't that help? Loads of it's junk mail, isn't it? Nobody'll care about that. That way, when the police arrive, at least it'll look like somebody made an effort. Like it wasn't all totally abandoned.'

I don't know how serious he was being. I think he only said it because somebody needed to say something, the silence was building, unbearable. But then I remembered the judge in Matthew Greenwood's trial. I had all those courtroom words memorised. *Among the items you attempted to destroy were irreplaceable family photographs and a present for a sick child* – singling those things out as really bad and deserving of extra-special punishment. If the equivalent important items in all *this* mail had been delivered, then that was one accusation that could never be made in court.

It'd be easy too, to separate the mail like that. You just looked at the postmark, the corporate logo, the way an item'd been addressed. Yes, those important items, if we could sort them, if there weren't *too* many of them . . .

'And because your mum's in hospital,' Daniel continued, 'the mitigating circumstances would be really strong, when it comes to court.'

Mitigating Circumstances, by the way, are what lawyers call having a Bloody Good Excuse. And the thing about excuses is sometimes they work, don't they?

'Court,' said Dad. 'Christ.'

'We've got to do it,' I said. 'Dad, what do you think? Dad?'

'There'll be too much.' He had his head up now facing us but the voice was the same dead-sounding one I'd heard him use when we drove to Tredegar House that time.

'At least we've got to *try*. Come on, Daniel.'

We went out to the garden, the two of us. Darkness was

coming on fast like it does in winter and the cloud from earlier was thinning so it looked like a clear sub-zero night lay ahead. Curtains were drawn up and down the terrace, nobody interested in looking out. Warm yellow windows, the soft bass murmur of televisions. Haxforth followed but he didn't join us when we went inside the shed and began gathering and carrying the armfuls of mail into the house. He stared up into the night sky, the big plastic lunchbox safe under his arm. A few stars were visible already. It didn't seem right asking him to do physical work, not after everything he'd been through.

The cold-slapping air brought a new urgency. Through the kitchen window I saw the microwave clock. 16.23. Little by little the shed emptied and the lounge filled up. Dad, staring into space, hadn't budged from the sofa.

When the mail was inside and the shed was a normal shed with old rusting tools and nothing else, Daniel and I began sorting.

One corner for the important stuff, the mail that really mattered. The letters from hospitals, letters of condolence, letters offering help. Cheques, passports, benefits, money needed. Red gas bills. Pay now or we'll cut you off, smack in the middle of winter. And within that corner, sorting into piles, putting everything into street and house order, like I'd been doing all along upstairs.

The rest of the room for the junk. Buy our pizzas. Win a holiday with our credit cards. Been turned down for a mortgage? Lose weight in the New Year. Life insurance, should a loved one die. Super-fast broadband. Special offers, a second pair of glasses half price. Buy this, get that for free. Dear valued customer . . .

'You've been going out, trying to deliver it yourself?' Dad said, after he'd watched us for a few minutes.

I nodded.

'How many times have you done that?'

'Don't know, lost count. Every morning . . .'

'In this weather,' he said to himself. 'Him too?'

'He just started helping me,' I said. 'That's Daniel. He's in my history class.'

Another couple of minutes went by in silence.

'You're doing it wrong,' Dad said. 'Spending too much time on the detail. Here, let me show you.'

He bent forward and grabbed a handful of mail and re-ordered it. His movements were stiff and jerky, robot-like, but still he was a lot faster at it than either of us.

Then he went down on all fours and took another handful and sorted it and then he arranged the piles into a better order and after that there were three of us working through this mass of mail, not two.

For a long while nobody spoke, only focused on what needed to be done.

'Most of it's junk anyway,' Daniel said at last, throwing aside yet another handful of envelopes.

'That's how Royal Mail makes most of their money these days,' Dad told him. 'Everybody knows it's rubbish. Not that that stops them telling us how important it is all the time.'

He seemed to be getting a bit more fluid now. The robot-jerkiness was gone and his face wasn't so white. 'Can't he help?' he said, looking into the kitchen and through to the window beyond where Haxforth's dark outline could just be made out in the garden.

'He can't read,' Daniel said. 'The names and addresses won't mean anything to him.'

'He can't *read*? What – at all?'

I shook my head.

'What is he, some homeless type?'

'Yeah.' It seemed easier, just saying that and nothing else.

'Why'd you do it, Aidan? Telling them he was your grandfather. Taking that bird in there. I don't get it. I don't understand why you'd do a thing like that.'

'I didn't mean it to happen! I thought . . .'

'Thought what?'

'I don't know,' I said miserably. 'I screwed up big time.'

'That makes two of us.' Dad put his hands together, pressed the joined-together fingertips to his mouth for a long moment. His eyes were closed, too. I don't really know what he was doing just then. Trying to pull everything in perhaps and make himself stronger somehow. Or making a wish, or deciding something. When he went back to the sorting, he attacked it like a demon.

At 18.28 I ran upstairs and hauled out the leftover mail from under my bed because we were nearly done. I didn't like the idea of the cops and Royal Mail investigators poking around my private space. Downstairs Dad was already bundling the mail, the important mail, together with red rubber bands. There was a lifetime's supply of those, littering the floor.

The piles were big – the neat organised batches. Maybe, *possibly*, they could be delivered before seven o'clock tomorrow morning. But the junk mail – no chance. Only by standing back rather than being on hands and knees among it could you appreciate how much there was. Then you got perspective. It was massive and mountainous, solid snowdrifts of mail, a cliff-face of piled-high post.

It could never be delivered on time.

Ignore it anyway and concentrate on the real stuff, the real mail that mattered to real people. Concentrate on those Mitigating Circumstances.

'We need our bikes,' I said to Daniel, thinking how stupid it'd been, leaving them back at Annandale Avenue.

I moved towards the door but Dad put a hand on my shoulder. He was standing up straighter than before. Haxforth was forgotten. What I'd done at the hospital was forgotten – or forgiven.

'I don't ever want you delivering post again in your life,' he said. 'Never, ever again.'

'There's too much for one person, you'll never do it . . .'

'Just help me get it in the car.'

'But what if someone sees you?'

Dad had his coat and bag on already – his winter Royal Mail gear. 'I'll have to risk it. If anyone asks, I'll roll my eyes and tell them it's Christmas overtime. Tonight's going to be the coldest night of the year anyway. That's what they've been saying on the radio. The streets'll be empty in an hour or two.'

You could see he wasn't going to change his mind.

We carried the bundles out to the car and arranged them geographically, on the back seat, on the front seat, in the boot, in the footwells. Then Dad took some black sacks out from under the kitchen sink and used them to cover the bundles over. No point asking for trouble, he said.

I stood by the gate with Daniel and watched him get into the car.

'Promise me one thing,' he said.

'What?'

'Promise you won't try to deliver any of that junk that's inside. Not one single item.'

'But—'

'It'll have to stay where it is. There's too much. I can't do anything about it and neither can you. I'll be here tomorrow morning, ready to face the music. That's what I should've done a long time ago.'

'Give us some of the real stuff then. We can do Annandale Avenue and round there.'

'No. I've got time, if I start now. You've done enough.' He turned the key in the ignition. 'Well?'

'I promise,' I muttered.

'And him?'

'I promise too.'

So then I knew it needed to be a real one, if Daniel said it.

'I'm sorry,' said Dad. 'About everything.'

He closed the door carefully.

The car made almost no sound as it drove into the night.

# 40

'Why did your father go to the trouble of stealing so much, if he wasn't going to open any of it?'

Haxforth motioned with his head through into the lounge. He was back inside the house, standing by the kitchen table. The lid of the plastic lunchbox was off and with one hand he was lining the inside with grass and twigs that must've come from our garden. The other he held flat against the open rim, to stop Old Beautiful escaping.

'He wasn't stealing it,' I told him. 'He just didn't deliver it.'

'Aidan's been trying to do that, but there's too much – what with Christmas and everything,' Daniel said.

'It's getting you into trouble, is that right?'

I nodded. Talk about understatement of the century.

We bent down, Daniel and me, peered into the lunchbox. Up close I saw how there were cracks in the skin of Haxforth's fingers. Lots of people get that in wintertime though, cracked skin.

*Old Magic*, that's what he'd said. *Old Magic made Old Beautiful and it made me.*

When? How?

Well, Old Beautiful wasn't looking too lively now, that was for sure. All the haywire energy from when it'd got loose in Mum's room was gone. The pustules on its face seemed to've dissolved or got soggy somehow, like when you do a painting in school but you use too much water and it runs. Its eyes were clear enough though and they were still sending out their black message BEWARE. In some way I couldn't understand it hardly even seemed to be a bird any more, more like some spectral presence, only halfway existing.

When he'd finished lining the lunchbox Haxforth snapped the lid with the stabbed-through air holes back into place. I looked at Daniel and he looked at me and I think we both felt relief, that thing being locked away safe.

Haxforth went through into the lounge and stared at the cliff-face of junk mail. So did I. That was the easy thing to do – just stare and stare and think about the amount of work needed to deliver it all. For a few minutes, when Dad had snapped back into life, I'd thought that maybe we could get out of this situation altogether. But now looking at it mountainous like the scrag-end of some volcanic explosion (and remembering how much Royal Mail valued this stuff), I knew there wasn't really any hope at all. The police were still going to arrest Dad, Mum was worse not better, I was heading direct for the nearest care home.

There'd been a time, once, when I'd honestly thought I could do something about it – the future, I mean. Thought

I could alter or affect it in some way, have some control. But now I saw it for what it was, an incoming meteor, red-burning, fierce-frictioned, undeflectable.

'You want to get rid of it?' Haxforth said.

'What do *you* think?'

He walked around the avalanche. Ran a hand through it. 'It's a pity,' he said. 'My brother would happily take it off your hands, but there's too much to carry, far too much.'

'You can't just dump it somewhere,' Daniel said. 'Sooner or later someone'll find it and . . .'

'Dumping? I wasn't proposing anything of the sort.'

'What were you proposing then?'

'Making it disappear. Forever. But look at it. If we had transport . . .'

I thought what a shame that was. A real crying shame in fact since we were going with him anyway, to find this long-lost brother of his.

Suddenly Daniel said, 'EX05 JYP.'

'What?'

He had the same expression on his face as when we'd skipped school that day of the museum. Only this time there was a load more fear. A load more excitement too.

'Christy's van. The Cloisters.'

'What's that got to do with . . . ?'

Then my brain made the connection.

'I can't believe you're even suggesting it,' I said.

'No, not *that* one. That'd be suicide. I just remembered seeing it earlier and, well – there must be others around like it.'

'I still don't believe it. *Any* van.' All the same I felt my stomach coasting like crazy because I knew right in that moment that we'd have to try it, had no choice.

'Haxforth,' I said, 'can you drive?'

'Why do you ask?'

I had to find out if that was a thing he could do before I got too excited myself. He never seemed to belong to the age of computers and machines. But really there was no way of knowing. If only you could take a slice out of him and count the rings, I thought, like you do with a tree.

Daniel and I told him what we had in mind.

'You mean a motorised getaway?' I saw the flicker of a smile, coffee-coloured tooth-stumps behind thin white lips. 'I believe I invented it.'

# 41

The moon was coming up already, leaving Maresfield Crescent behind. It shone out over the rooftops like a big beaming spotlight. So much for my alliance. Where was the cloud when you needed it, the cloud that buried the light away the whole rest of the time? As we walked I handed Daniel a dark woollen scarf, one of two I'd taken from Mum's room. The last thing we wanted, if we really were going to do this thing, was to be seen and identified – it being a small town with everyone knowing everyone else, or at least that's how it seemed a lot of the time. Right away Daniel tied it tight, pulled it high over his mouth and nose. That was a good thing to do anyway. The cold came at you from everywhere, like being nipped at by a thousand icy pincers.

Haxforth hovered alongside, moving in and out of my field of vision. Most people his age'd never set foot outside on a night like this. The blood must pump slower by then and not reach certain parts of the body so well. Maybe the skin and bones start thinning too. But there he was, keeping up – Old Beautiful left safe behind in our kitchen – and sometimes you hardly even saw him, thanks to that silent shadowy way he had of moving.

I had a destination in mind, a specific destination. First though another place worth checking out, a courier van that was always parked nearby. Even as I thought it, the house came into view. With scarves up and hoods down Daniel and I stepped in closer. The van was ideal, but the Neighbourhood Watch sticker in the lighted house window wasn't. Someone was moving around inside there too. This guy'd be dialling 999 in about two seconds flat. Concealed faces wouldn't help much if police cars came out looking for us. Straightaway we moved on.

Our big chance lay four streets on. There was almost nobody about, one or two figures only hurrying by with heads down. Dad, or the radio, must've been right about this being the coldest night of the year. House after house after house and all the roads endless it seemed. Finally we saw it, the vehicle I'd noticed many times and which I knew'd be empty since it was part of a removals business. It was parked kerbside and for a moment, drawing closer, thinking this was possible, I heard the blood-drums start up in my head.

Then, 'It's boxed right in,' Daniel said. 'Look at it.'

He was right. Standing parallel in the middle of the road I saw how everything was bumper to bumper. Unless one of the neighbouring cars shifted first, it'd be impossible to manoeuvre out.

'This was actually a pretty stupid idea. Perhaps we should head back . . .'

'You were the one who thought of it,' I said.

'It just came out. When you stop to think about—'

Quickly Haxforth pushed us away. There was a curtain twitching, a face peering from a nearby window.

There were others, seen and identified as we roamed the frozen streets: one that looked perfect until a blinding halogen snapped on from an adjacent house, another that when Haxforth opened it up was full of timber . . . You *think* there are vans everywhere, but when you start looking for them, there really aren't. At least there weren't that night, not ones we could use anyway.

We kept moving though. Daniel didn't say anything more about going back to Maresfield Crescent. By then we all knew exactly where we were headed. It was like fate or something was leading us right there.

The Cloisters are those new-builds, one snail-shaped street interlocking inside others and all the houses like neat square boxes. The place looks like it's dropped out of a cereal packet. But standing on its corner we saw every door fortressed now against the winter. Double glazing everywhere. That was good, it'd help deaden noise from the street.

The van stood on a brick-paved driveway, its windows icing over already. Daniel had been right, there was no doubting it belonged to Christy. Even without the registration plate I'd've recognised it, the battered-up bodywork that made it so different to all the other smart silver cars parked on the street.

'What do you think?' I whispered.

'I'm not sure . . .'

'The thing is, he won't go running to the cops, will he? So if we can get it away from here, there's zero comeback.'

Daniel pushed his scarf higher, almost covering his eyes. 'It doesn't *look* like anybody's in . . .'

'Haxforth, what do you think?'

I saw a nod, a wisp of breath on the night air.

'Let's do it,' I said.

We worked it like this. The three of us shadow-creeping up the driveway even though the moon was glaring down supercharged. Everything dark inside the box-like house. Ears straining to hear beyond curtained windows, difficult to pick up sound however what with the blood-drums beating time again.

Christy, who'd attacked Haxforth. Christy who'd bought the chains and padlocks, who'd picked out the place to keep him prisoner. Was he inside, right now? Or out somewhere, twisting elbows, fixing on the next opportunity?

I watched Haxforth slip a hand under the black plastic handle, heard a soft metallic *clunk* as the door opened and he climbed in behind the steering wheel. He'd told us he could steal a vehicle fine and this was fast work sure enough. Daniel and I, we got around to the front. As soon as Haxforth took the handbrake off we'd push the van backwards down the little inclined hardstanding and out into the road and then try to get it turned, try for some momentum and distance till it felt safe to switch on the engine. It'd be insane doing it too close to the house, especially if Haxforth needed a few attempts to get the thing started. He was so old, so dried-up and such a bad fit with the twenty-first century that part of me couldn't help wondering if he really could drive at all.

Behind the dark glass of the windscreen I saw a hand rise and swipe down. That was the signal.

I didn't look at Daniel but I could feel him pushing alongside me. Pushing and heaving with legs and arms braced, using the whole of the earth underfoot to take the strain, knowing the trick was just to get that first turn, half-turn, quarter-turn even, out of the wheels and then we'd be fine or on our way at least.

'Come *on*!' I heard Daniel whisper through closed teeth.

A slight silent lurch and the white mass started to roll. Inch by inch it moved, metre by metre. Picking up speed. We kept with the speed, tried to increase it. Already Haxforth was turning the wheel so the van'd get out into the road right.

Suddenly it was rolling too fast. Then it was *really* rolling too fast. Perhaps Haxforth was stepping on the clutch instead of the brake. Not exactly a good omen for our motorised getaway if he was. Daniel and I ran down alongside trying to slow and steady the van but it was like stopping a new-christened ship on the slipway. Use the brake, use the brake, we tried to tell him by waving our arms.

The van hit the dip between driveway and road and as it did so the exhaust pipe crunched lightly on the tarmac. In the cold still night the sound seemed to reverberate around the world.

The van came to a stop.

Inside the house, upstairs, a light flicked on.

'Get it moving again!' I hissed at Daniel. 'Get it straightened up, so he can start the engine!'

Already I was thinking, Jesus Christ and bloody hell we've had it and we can't even run, not really, because then we'd be leaving Haxforth there in the cab where Christy'd be pleased enough to see him again, no worries about that, and what the hell did we think we were playing at?

'Just bloody *push*!'

'I *am* pushing!' Daniel said.

Under my hands I felt the bonnet rattle as the engine flooded with loud mechanical power. We hadn't agreed on this, not starting the engine so near. I had no idea how Haxforth was doing it, whether he was hotwiring or whatever, but it didn't catch, just turned over and died. Again he tried and I tried to get his attention through the windscreen, telling him to stop, but he was a dark hunched figure not noticing. Instinctively me and Daniel stepped away from the van, not knowing whether to climb in or stay on the street. For a third time Haxforth tried the engine and this time the mechanics sounded louder and even more painful and the van jumped forward so you knew he didn't even have it in neutral and everything was going wrong and it was all the most terrible mistake.

Then I saw a dark rectangle where the front door of Christy's house had been.

A shout came through the night. You couldn't hear what the shout said but you knew what it meant all right and you could hear the salt and scabs in the throat. A snarling leaping face came in close and already Christy had Daniel down on the ground and he was kicking him and I knew right then it was that moment you always wonder about, how you'll handle it, pure animal survival.

I got my hands up, the stone-hard fist-blocks high and full of top velocity and I charged. Daniel was curled into a tight protective ball. No-one else had come out of the house, it was just me and Christy and after all he was only human, a human like me who could be damaged, and he saw me and put his own hands up but it was too late, I smashed through and I have never hit anyone as hard as that and for a second he looked astonished then I heard the *slubb* as he fell and his head hit the cold concrete kerb.

Behind me I heard the engine catch and establish. The passenger door flew open and I saw the tip of a hand waving at us to get inside. I yanked Daniel to his feet and he was hyperventilating but there wasn't any time to stop because Christy was moving around, trying to get up, a wounded animal which everyone knows are the most dangerous and now he was on his feet and staggering after us but we were up to the van that was moving past and I was shoving Daniel in head first, into the front passenger seat next to Haxforth who wasn't anything more than a dark outline and then me in beside him, my hands reaching and searching for the inside door handle, desperate to get it shut, get it locked, get safe.

A kick went into the back of the van. Vicious intent but no proper connection, because by then we were lurching away and the Cloisters was behind us.

# 42

Through the streets. Left, right, left, left, wishing Maresfield Crescent was zones away. Daniel looked pale and waxy when he took his scarf off but at least it hadn't come loose at all. There was no danger of Christy ever picking him out from a crowd. And his eyes were fine, sharp and paying attention and not glazed over, so I knew there was nothing fundamental to worry about.

'Thanks,' he said after a painful minute or two.

'No problem.' I didn't really feel like talking about it. There was a big part of me that still felt bad about the things I'd done to him at school, back when I'd needed his dinner money. Maybe rescuing him like that would make up for some of it. Not that I did it *because* of that. Both of us knew what Christy would've done to him if I hadn't got in there. All that was unspoken but understood.

I watched him rub his back, massage his thigh, check the

matchbox in his jeans pocket where he kept the arrowhead clasp.

'The last time I was in this vehicle, I was locked in the back,' Haxforth said. 'Satisfying, stealing it tonight.'

'You hotwired it?' Daniel sounded impressed.

'It's no great skill. The problem was the pedals – so sensitive. Kept popping out from under my feet. But it's all coming naturally now.'

Right, left. Right, right. Into Maresfield Crescent. Haxforth pulled in, killed the lights and engine and we sat for a moment looking up and down the road. Most of the houses still had their lights on, walls and gardens pearled by the moon.

It was now. Or it was never.

The winter freeze made a snatch for the air in my lungs as I stepped out of the van. Haxforth and Daniel were with me. Up the path to the house we went, through the passageway gate with the clicking closing hinge. Into the kitchen where we'd left Old Beautiful, unmoved in its locked-down plastic nest.

From under the sink I took out the roll of black sacks. It was a good thick roll and there was a second one behind it, a reminder of bulk-buying in the supermarket back when we did normal family things like that together. It was good, having that second roll, since we were going to need them all. One after another I tore them off, walloped them through the air to get them open. In the lounge Daniel was already shovelling handfuls of mail.

'Big bags and darkness,' Haxforth said. 'The two things every thief needs.'

Five, six, seven bags we filled, Haxforth holding open the mouths of the sacks while Daniel and I rammed and compacted the mail. Me tying the bags and stacking them out in the passageway. I saw Haxforth take an envelope and turn it over in his hands, feel it, begin to open the flap. The cracks in his skin were getting more noticeable. They seemed to be all over his body now, all the bits of it I could see anyway.

'There's no point,' I told him. 'There's nothing in it, all of this is rubbish.'

'All of it?'

'Yeah. And we don't have time to mess around.'

'Oh well,' he said. 'Force of habit. It's utterly pointless anyway.'

Then one of the bags split because we'd overfilled it and after that we didn't talk any more but double-bagged instead because wherever it was we were taking all this mail, whatever it was that Haxforth's brother was going to do with it (if we ever found him), the last thing we wanted was a telltale trail of white and brown envelopes left behind like breadcrumbs in the fairy tale. After about the twentieth sackload I stopped counting, just kept shovelling and compacting and tying the bags and stacking them outside.

'Last one,' Daniel whispered finally. 'How many is that, altogether?'

'God knows.' I glanced into the kitchen. The clock on the microwave said 21.41. How had it got to be so late? I checked my torch, maybe I wouldn't need it with the moon so full and the sky so clear but you never knew. Carrying it was automatic by then anyway. There are always places where moonlight never falls, murky places where shadows lie solid like black concrete. Perhaps it was one of those places we were headed for now.

One last look around the house, one last look in the shed too, making certain we'd got every single item, picturing in my mind all the while tomorrow morning's scene, the Royal Mail investigators and their police cronies stepping from warm cars. But they'd all be too late. The house was just a house and the shed an ordinary garden shed, with tins of old paint and rusted tools and offcuts of wood and nothing else.

Haxforth came up behind me while I was shining the torch inside there. I watched a hand reach past my shoulder, take down a spade hanging from a rusted nail. A minute or so later I saw him sitting in the driver's seat of the van, ready to go.

I stared at the piles of black sacks in the passageway.

'Let's get them in,' I said to Daniel.

Silent as behind-the-lines commandos we started hauling. The back doors of the van were unlocked so we just slung them in there, faster and faster and faster. Suddenly it felt like we couldn't afford to waste another single second. The windows of the houses all around were closed and curtained, but all it would take was one to blink open because it looked dodgy as hell what we were doing. Quickly the dank space in the back of the van filled up until we were having to kick and cram and shove and ram just to get it all in. The final three bags we stuffed onto the front passenger seat out of desperation.

Haxforth didn't say anything and he didn't offer to help. I knew Old Beautiful would be in there with him somewhere, the creature that seemed to have been like a hideous companion to him all those long years of his life.

'You sit in the front,' I told Daniel when we'd run around and got everything like we wanted it.

'What about you? There isn't room for all three of us . . .'

'I'll burrow in the back. Just make sure you close the door properly after me.'

I tunnelled in among the sacks, heard the doors slam. Already the engine was starting up.

'Comfortable?' I heard Daniel ask from the front.

'No,' I said.

'Are there any seatbelts back there?'

'Having a laugh, aren't you? It's difficult enough just breathing.'

I felt the van slide along empty roads. Ten minutes later we were leaving town.

Time to meet Haxforth's mysterious brother.

# 43

We drove. Through tiny gaps in the body-pressing bags I glimpsed road lights, familiar green signs. With a bit of struggle-and-twist I got myself squatted behind the headrests up in the front of the van. The bags still crowded in tight but at least here I could see where we were going. The sodium lamps dangling above the tarmac made the three of us look tired and shadowy. Somewhere Haxforth pulled off, bumped over a mini-roundabout and we left the lights behind. Quietly, without saying a word, Daniel took out his phone and I watched him turn it off, watched the screen go dead. Dark lanes now, no pavements, the road twisting this way and that. Plunging on and on, the headlights switched to high beam, two white funnels speeding ahead of us. The moon glided and kept pace above, one of those nights where you can't believe it only reflects and doesn't generate light. Was this the way Haxforth had been coming when he'd run into Christy and his pals?

'Where are we?' I said. 'I've never been out this way before. I don't recognise any of it.'

No answer. On we flew, turning, twisting, eating up tarmac. The road signs were flashing by too fast now for us to read them. They were the old-fashioned sort, black letters on white pointers, all words and numbers blurred.

'I recognise that signpost,' Daniel said after a time. 'The way it's half fallen over. We went by here ten minutes ago. We're lost, aren't we?'

'Not lost,' Haxforth told him. 'Circling.'

He shot me a look in the rear-view mirror. Shadows cast by a line of roadside trees slid across his ghostly face. 'I know this stretch,' I heard him say quietly.

Know it? I thought. How? From these endless grass verges and hedges and country lanes, all looking the same and not a single distinctive thing to tell them apart?

Suddenly he said, 'There,' and slammed down on the brakes so the bags surged up around me and he was reversing along the patched and peeling tarmac, swinging the van through an angle and in the headlights now there stood a rusted gate and beyond it a track, farmland it looked like but rising, at least as far as we could see.

Haxforth whispered something to Daniel, and Daniel got out and opened the gate, holding it wide so we could drive through and then he closed the gate behind us and climbed back in.

The track was white. Everything that night was white, luminous, ivory-coloured. It was like all the real colours in the world had got sucked away so you didn't know if they'd ever come back and would red, green or blue ever mean anything again. The van crunched along the track, over lumps that looked in the headlights like badly buried bones. I was getting a ride in the back all right, the smoothness of the road gone and everything thumping up and down, grabbing onto anything I could find for support.

Up we went and up. At a place where the ground levelled out, Haxforth stopped and wound down the window and looked out. In the moonlight I saw how the cracks in his skin were worse than ever. Some lights twinkled down below, distant lights from the regular world.

'I'm going to release Old Beautiful,' he said.

'Is it going to show us the way to Shuttle Hill?'

I said that because sometimes it seems to me that even *ordinary* birds know things we don't, the way they move so easy and not being held down by guilty churning brains like us. And then *this* bird, this ancient swallow returned in midwinter with Haxforth, well, there was nothing too ordinary or everyday about that at all.

'We'll see.'

I watched Haxforth lift the big plastic lunchbox from the place where he'd stored it in the front of the van. He laid it on his lap and unclipped and removed the lid.

'If it goes for your head, make sure to beat it away.'

'Thanks for the warning.'

Old Beautiful unfolded its wings and moved its scaly lumpen feet. In the moonlight and shadow it looked congealed and matted like those birds you see on TV when they get caught in an oil slick. It even seemed to move like oil somehow, sort of fluid and flowing, as it lifted clear of the plastic nest and made the short hop to the open window ledge of the van.

'Poor swallow.' Haxforth stroked its feathers. 'He's had his own burden to carry all these years.'

In the frozen silence I could hear its tiny bird heart beat-beating madly fast. Could it even fly at all any more? But even as I had the thought it was a dark flicker escaping over a nearby hedge.

Abruptly Haxforth put the van into gear and crashed through after it.

Bushes flared and crumpled in the headlights. We were in a field of some sort, regular patterns streaming by in the earth below. Now I was really hanging on. A glance told me Daniel was braced up too, legs wedged against the dashboard and arms up around his head like a protective doughnut. His face looked grim, a crash-test dummy for real. At least he had a seatbelt which was more than I could say.

'Poor swallow. Poor Haxforth.'

That ride couldn't last forever. We were going faster and faster, downhill now unexpectedly and picking up even more speed and either the van was going to break or we were. But still the shock when it came, the scream from Daniel, the sensation of flying, the twisting metal as we crashed, was deep-gut sickening, pure flashback material. For a freeze-frame moment I even thought we were going to roll and then the petrol tank'd blow like you see in the films.

Instead the engine died and the van rocked to a halt.

Outside, silence.

We sat and listened to it. Nobody wanted to escape the wreckage just yet. Deep deep quiet, the only sounds coming from within our bodies, the inside noises that tell you you're still alive.

'What happened?' I said, hardly even knowing my own voice above the blood slamming in ears and throat.

'God. Oh god.' For a moment I saw Daniel with his face

pressed hard against the windscreen. He turned mechanical and doll-like, his face like a stiff white mask. 'I think we drove into a ditch.'

'Are you all right? Anything broken?'

'I'm . . . I'm OK.' He moved some more, felt and tested his body and I saw how the seatbelt had held him in place, stopped him from being hurled through the windscreen. With me in the back though it was only the way the mail had pitched up, a split-second barricade of soft protection against the head-rests, that had come between my body and a headlong artery-slicing death.

I breathed slow and deep, filled my lungs, tried not to think about it. Dad's stolen mail had saved my life. It was what you might call an irony – one of those things adults laugh at all the time and feel clever doing it, saying something like How Completely Typical. Maybe it would feel funny to me too, later on. But it didn't right then.

'Where's Haxforth?' Suddenly I saw how the driver's seat was empty, the door levered partway open. 'He's not here.'

'Up there . . .' Daniel said.

The shock of the accident must have done something to my head, to how it worked out times and distances, because once I'd kicked my way clear of the nosedived van and splashed through the icy water at the bottom of the drainage ditch and scrambled up the bank, the ghostly figure of Haxforth was disappearing into a line of woodland and he seemed to be about half a mile away already.

'What's going on?' Daniel whispered, pale and breathless beside me.

Haxforth stopped, turned. Down by his feet I saw the black square shape of the spade he'd taken from the shed. It was easy, seeing all that. The moon-ceiling and the frost-carpet threw light off each other. He waved an arm at us. The gesture was unmistakable. It said, Follow, follow.

'Do you think we should?' You could tell just by looking how much the crash had shaken Daniel. It would have shaken anybody. But to think of turning round now, of going home? Apart from anything else there was all that mail in the back of the van. No way could we leave it there, abandoned at the bottom of some farmer's ditch.

'Come on,' I said. 'We'll lose sight of him otherwise.'

We ran, Daniel and I, ran to catch up. The trees were nearer than they looked and through them I saw that Haxforth was limping. Had he been injured in the crash? On into the woods where twigs and branches glittered with frost. I could almost see the crystals growing one on top of another, spinning their furry points, their patterns of ice.

The trees thinned and stopped. Haxforth was waiting for us there. We were standing on the edge of a little valley set into the hillside. Not that it was a proper geography-definition valley, more like a long dip or scar in the landscape. Still somehow it felt like a high-up sort of place, a sky-pressing place. Perhaps that was because of the way the moon filled the sky. But the moon wasn't the brightest thing in that place, not by a long way. There was something else giving off light. You could've seen it miles away, a super-bright beacon. Or, I don't know, maybe nobody ever saw it but us.

'Shuttle Hill,' Haxforth said.

# 44

You know how it is on Bonfire Night, lighting a sparkler and waving it around, making shapes in the air? How you see the trails left behind, burned into your vision? Well, think of that effect, multiply it, add zeros at the end. That'll give you a good idea.

An apple tree stood at the centre of this little valley, this sky-pressing scar. Full grown, thick with glossy leaves, hung with fruit. And from top to bottom it glowed and burned like the after-image of a sparkler, or maybe like something erupted from the deep molten parts of the earth, the magma we never think about while we're walking around every day on the cold forgettable crust. But there was no fizz or crackle to it, it was silent, completely, eerily silent.

Straightaway I wished I'd never seen it because it was an impossible thing and I knew it'd haunt me forever. It wouldn't help too much with trying to forget the doctor on the radio and what he'd said that time, how I might inherit Mum's condition and end up hearing things one day and seeing them too. Mild hallucinations, to begin with. Auditory and visual.

Like there was anything mild about *this.*

Old Beautiful circled the tree, not dark any more like oil or shadow but more like a shard of flying flaring magnesium.

'All round here,' Haxforth said softly, 'all around – there were orchards.'

I went nearer to the tree. Daniel beside me was doing the same. Thank god he's here to see this, I thought. Thank god it isn't just me. Coming up close, seeing the patterns in the bark, you felt you could almost get lost in it, be at one with the tree somehow. I don't know what it was really or how to describe it except to say there was a sort of stillness in there that moved. It ran like bright rivers in the clefts and crevices of the tree. Words can't capture it. Words don't come anywhere near. But you knew if you put your hand into that running stillness, it would take you somewhere. I don't know where exactly. And then everything inside would be peaceful and green, or blue, only you might not ever be able to leave. Once you were in it. You might not want or be able to leave it behind and return to the world of houses and cars and schools.

I glanced across at Daniel, saw him wide- and glassy-eyed, knew he was thinking all this too.

The light didn't seem to affect Haxforth at all. I shaded my eyes, turned with an effort away from the silent firework tree, watched him poking around in the undergrowth a little off to one side. He was definitely limping, moving with difficulty. You could hear every sound he made, every breath that seemed suddenly to be a wheeze, every straining spade-scrape.

*Chnnck.*

He raised the metal blade over a bulging scrubby place and brought it down. Did it again, cut the soil, started to dig.

*Chnnck. Chnnck. Chnnck.*

I pulled Daniel away from the tree. Some of its bright hypnotising life seemed to be dimming already. Together we watched Haxforth work the spade.

'What's he doing?' Daniel whispered. 'What's he digging for?'

Haxforth looked up. Looked direct at us. The thin combed hair, the winter coat. He might have been any old bloke turning the soil at his allotment. Only the cracked skin gave him away. And those eyes. White, not yellow or bloodshot, but still the tiredest eyes I'd ever seen. He grunted something and bent his head and drove the spade down into the earth again.

*Chnnck! Chnnck! Chnnck!*

'Hey,' I said, going over to join him, kicking at the displaced soil. 'It's soft. This is almost mud! But – everywhere else is frozen solid . . .'

The metal blade flew down, rebounded with a dull clang.

Hitting stone.

A slab. Hidden under the earth, cracked down the middle. The crack must have been there before, no spade could have made an impact like that. Haxforth got down on his hands and knees to scrabble the mud away and so did I.

We lifted one half of the slab away. Daniel helping with the other. Underneath there was a deep black hole. No moonlight reached down there, none of the fading apple-tree light either. Haxforth was puffing and blowing and his skin looked like paper that'd been crumpled and then smoothed out.

He rocked back on his heels, steadied himself with those thin white hands.

'This is where it happened.'

'Where *what* happened?' Daniel said.

'The Old Magic. The ceremony. One thousand years ago.'

I glanced back at the tree. The light was almost gone now. It really was like that experiment at school, igniting the magnesium strip – burns so bright and dies so fast. Its branches had drooped and the apples themselves were gone, fallen into the frost underfoot perhaps or disappeared somehow in the white heatless blaze.

'If either of you boys has a torch,' Haxforth muttered, 'please, switch it on.'

There were tears on his cheeks, I saw now, silvery threads from moon-swamped eyes.

I took my torch out of my pocket and flicked it on. Daniel had one too, did the same. We shone the beams down into the hole.

There were some old grey pots and a rust-eaten sword.

There was gold. There was lots of gold.

There was a long dusty skeleton.

'My brother,' Haxforth said. 'My king.'

# 45

'*That's* your brother?' I heard myself say. 'But he must be – you must be – *centuries* ago . . .'

'We were born athelings,' Haxforth said. 'Both of us. No ordinary nobles though. Royalty. For a long time I didn't understand what that meant, not properly. We grew up laughing, that's how I remember it. All our lives spent in sunshine. Then everything changed. One minute we were climbing trees. The next they were putting a crown on his head.'

'They?'

'The other nobles. The heads of families, those who called themselves thanes or earls. He was too young for it, far too young. Everyone knew. It was what they wanted, you see, what they'd planned for – their chance to control the sovereign, the highest authority in the land. But how can you influence someone who listens only to the voices inside their head?'

I thought of Mum, of how the last time I'd seen her the

flickering-inside-candle that was her real life had looked like it might go out forever. 'I know what that feels like,' I said, but so quietly I knew Haxforth hadn't heard.

'The signs were there before he came to the throne. When he was what you would call a teenager. Only afterwards did it worsen. How it worsened. And something like that, it can't be hidden forever. Gossip starts, word gets out. The healers could do nothing for him. The priests had no answers. "Pray for him," – that was all they could say. What use was that? If a king is ruined, his kingdom perishes with him. Crops, cattle, people – everything withers. The land dies, or lies open to invasion.'

Haxforth's face edged into darkness, closer to the mouth of the pit. In the moonlight I saw earth crushed hard between the fingers of his cold-clawed hands.

'There was a belief in those times: if evil lived inside a person, a disease or an illness, it had to be driven out. Cut out and removed. It couldn't be discarded afterwards, however. Disease can't ever be destroyed, not completely. It needs to be received by another creature – transplanted into them and carried safely away. That creature becomes a living sacrifice. Ordinarily an animal was used, but if the person was important, or the disease untreatable, something more was needed. Something of greater worth. And should a terrible affliction be visited upon the most important person of all, then the vessel, the sacrifice, had to be human. Someone of high status. A member of the same family.'

'The same family?' Daniel's voice was hushed. 'You mean – *you*?'

'The younger brother. Still a child on the night they took me from my bed.'

I flashed the torch across Haxforth's face and wished straightaway that I hadn't, pointed the beam right back down the hole. It would have been cruel, shining any more light on that face. It was too exhausted, too far gone with sadness and regret.

'It was forbidden, even then. The papal religion was everywhere, the religion of the Christ figure. But still there were certain people, certain individuals travelling secretly, men who could be found if they were needed. Someone, somewhere, made the decision – petition the Old Magic at midsummer. Drive out the madness. They were waiting for me here. *He* was waiting for me here.'

'Something like that . . . it isn't possible.'

'I've never stopped seeing his face. The magician. The scars striping his body and the feathers and dirt in his hair. He wore a necklace of apples, whole apples, down to his knees. He was like a star fallen to earth. You only had to look into his eyes to know that. Someone who could reach deep into life's pulse and turn it any way he wanted. A true monster – the only one I ever met.'

'But the tree – and Old Beautiful . . .' Daniel said.

'The things he used. The tools he reached for at midsummer. The swallow was inside an iron cage, a cage with a circular door, just large enough for a human head. We knelt before it, my brother and I. The cage went first to him. Later in the night it came to me.'

'Jesus,' I said. 'You had to put your head in?'

'There were arms holding us everywhere.'

'So Old Beautiful acted sort of like an amplifier,' murmured Daniel. 'Or a gutter, carrying away dirty water . . .'

'They released it afterwards. They didn't care what happened to it then. It had served its purpose.' Haxforth gazed down into the pit where our torch beams were still crossing. 'So had I. They led me away as the sun came up. The king stood piled high with apple blossom. That was the last time I saw him.'

'Until tonight . . .'

'Until tonight. One thousand years. The span of time they deemed necessary to protect against any return of the madness.'

A sort of shuddering sound spilled out from Haxforth's throat and for a moment I thought – well, I don't know what I thought. But all that'd happened was the tears had stopped filling up his eyes. I saw that clearly enough. Perhaps there weren't any more to come, ever. How could a body keep living that long anyway? How could all the muscles and chemicals and liquids, all the important inside stuff, keep on moving forever like the sea?

'The heads of families, the thanes and earls, they agreed it among themselves. A request was made – and granted. I've been living all this time because men with the power to decide happened to think that was a nice safe number. A satisfying number.'

*In such cases the public expects a custodial sentence*, I thought. *Today that is what I am giving you.*

'But what happened afterwards?' Daniel said. 'To you, I mean?'

'Oh, they sent me away with gold. A few trinkets to pay me off – their way of easing the guilt. As if such objects could do anything but endanger a child alone on the road. I trusted the first person who treated me kindly, and by nightfall bandits were hunting me down. Criminals happy to kill for a single gold coin. There was nowhere to go, no-one to turn to. I ran, went deeper and deeper into the wild, cried myself to sleep.

When I woke up the moon was high and full, just as it is now – and there was Old Beautiful, watching me. That's when I understood we were linked somehow, both of us cursed by that ceremony. I sealed the trinkets into a cleft in some rocks, hoping to come back for them in a week or two . . .'

'The clasp?' I said. 'And the bracelet Christy took . . . ?'

Haxforth nodded. 'Perhaps that was part of the magic – the beginning of my exile. Some doors closed, others opened. All of them led away from here. The chance came for a place on a ship across the Channel. It was nostalgia that made me look for those things again, at the end. Curiosity. Nothing more.'

I closed my eyes. My brain felt dead and flattened out. I couldn't think this through now. If it had been Mum telling me about kings and magicians and creepy midsummer ceremonies, I wouldn't have believed the first word. But this was Haxforth. It *felt* real. Scary, but real. And wasn't the evidence all around us?

'And you've been a thief *all this time*?' Daniel said.

Haxforth smiled and the skin around his mouth and eyes seemed to crackle as he did so. 'I was brought up an atheling – no-one ever showed me how to work the land. Stealing was something I discovered a talent for.'

Slowly, carefully, not moving too easily, he dangled an arm towards the skeleton. His hand was shaking like a kite in strong wind. There was no way he was going to reach it though, it was too far down.

'Swallows go over the water, you see. Always moving, never settling. Apple trees stay where they are, bountiful, growing roots, casting a protective canopy . . .'

I followed his gaze. All that gold lying there. I knew it was important, but somehow my torch beam kept getting dragged back to the skull which had rolled a little to one side. The dirt lay thick in its mouth and eyeholes. A row of teeth gleamed like Scrabble tiles on a rack.

'Didn't you ever hear them? If you were carrying them, the voices, like you said – didn't you ever hear them?'

'Not in the way he did. Or maybe they came, only one after another – one life after another. There's been so much of that. Too, too much.'

For a long time none of us said anything. Haxforth's eyes were so far back in his head and empty of life now that they weren't much more than sockets, dead volcano craters. Overhead the moon throbbed, throbbed fierce against my flatlining brain.

'I'd like to sit under the apple tree one last time.'

So that's what we did. He could hardly move at all by then so Daniel and I got him under the arms and carried him across to the tree. We did it all solemn and gentle and he weighed almost nothing. The tree was dead, cold, a peeling husk. Old Beautiful, Haxforth's strange companion during his long magical exile, had vanished.

'We're the final echoes,' he said into my ear, as we got him comfortable against the trunk. 'After today, after tonight, the Old Magic won't ever move in this world again.'

'But Haxforth, what about the mail? What do I do with it?'

'Isn't it obvious?'

I thought about it and yes, it was obvious.

I touched Daniel on the shoulder, pointed the way out of the little valley. It wasn't like there was anything more we could do for Haxforth. We both knew what was going to happen and it didn't feel right, hanging around. Felt like a massive intrusion.

Through the trees, back to the drainage ditch and the wreck

of the van. Stay strong, I told myself that whole time. Remember what we're here for. Getting rid of the mail, keeping Dad out of prison. It was a fight to get the back doors open but we did it. One bag each, shoulder-slung or front-carried, whatever came easiest. Lucky it was downhill because each one seemed to weigh a tonne now, far heavier than they'd been back at the house. We stacked the bags besides the burial chamber, turned for the next lot.

Hill. Trees. Van. Bags, carry, stack. For a long time we did that and nothing else and all the time I tried not to look over at Haxforth, still propped unmoving against the trunk of the apple tree. After a while it was like even Daniel wasn't there any more. He was a shadow that happened to be tagging along, fading away. The black sacks were agony in my hands. All I wanted to do was stop and rest, but I didn't, I kept fetching them, hauling them, putting one foot in front of the other, just doing that and nothing else over and over and over again. Each delivery made me feel light as a butterfly when I dropped it, like I might lift into the night sky and never come down – then came the turn and the climb and the agony starting all over again.

Frost thickened over everything, over Haxforth, frost so thick it was almost snow.

Finally I knew I had to go and look at him properly. Only a single bag was left in the van then and Daniel must've been up there, he wasn't with me anyhow, it was only me and Haxforth in that moment. His skin, when I went close, made me think of the tectonic plates we'd learned about in geography. These plates of his were tiny, no bigger than thumbnails, but still they seemed to have shifted or cracked apart. And that right then was probably the single saddest thing I ever saw in my life, even including everything that had happened with Mum, because somehow in that moment he wasn't Haxforth any more but everyone who had ever lived and struggled and died, which was everyone ever and would be me too one day. And what made it ten times worse even than that was the way his body was curled in the long icy grass with his chin down by his chest and arms tucked in tight. Because that shape was exactly the same as my favourite sleeping position every night, the position I always felt safest in.

# 46

A noise over by the grave-mouth told me Daniel'd made it down with that final load. All the rest were in position and ready to go.

'The bag split,' he said. 'The mail went everywhere. I was really careful picking it up though. I don't think I missed any.'

'Thanks,' I said, meaning it.

'I think my fingers have gone black. I can hardly feel them any more.'

'Haxforth's dead.'

Daniel nodded and together we went and stood over the old white body. What do you do in a situation like that? Do you say something, ashes to ashes, put something over his face? If there are rules about that kind of stuff, I don't know what they are.

A breeze ruffled the frozen grass-tips around his body. The breeze strengthened, turned into a wind. Something else was rising too, through the cracks in his skin, the same thing I'd seen oozing from the shrunken tree back at Annandale Avenue. The death-poison that had stayed away so long.

'Come on.' I bent down, ready to heave the body towards the grave-mouth.

'You're going to touch him?' Daniel said. 'Like that? Are you sure?'

'No. But we can't leave him here, can we?'

I grabbed the body around the chest and then Daniel leaned in too and we pulled Haxforth across the sky-pressing landscape, gouging a black line in the whiteness underfoot. Somehow he felt slippery and powdery at the same time, I don't know why that should've been.

'What are we going to do, just tip him in?' asked Daniel when we reached the edge of the pit.

'Try to lower him, I reckon.'

Somehow we got him upright and cantilevered all correct so he'd go down feet first. The hole was deep but not that wide so it was going to be a tricky operation whichever way you looked at it, and then when you thought of what needed to go in afterwards you wondered if it was all going to fit. But with the skeleton down there, you knew this was the only way it could end. The only problem was, we were going to have to drop him at some point. It didn't matter how delicate we were, that was inevitable. And with the shaft being so narrow, there was a good chance he'd fold or block it up somehow. If *that* happened, we'd never get everything else in, it'd be impossible.

I let Daniel take the weight for a moment and laid on my front, beside the stone slab buried all those hundreds of years. A white worm crinkled along its earthy underside. How far down exactly was the bottom? I scanned with the torch, made a careful examination, tried with determination to keep my eyes away from the hypnotising skull and surrounding gold. It was deep but not deep enough that if you jumped it'd kill you. There was a place off to the side, I saw now, an unfilled space or second chamber of some kind. If we could get Haxforth in there then everything else'd work out no problem. Maybe, I thought, that second chamber had even been left empty on purpose, back in those brutal times.

What it meant, though, was that to get his cracked-up lightweight body into its final resting place, one of us was going to have to go *down there* and pull it into position.

I got back on my feet and told Daniel what I was going to do. I didn't wait to hear what he had to say about it. He'd have objections. What if the walls collapse, what if you can't get back out, you'll be buried alive, suffocated, then there'll be two bodies to deal with, three if you count that old dead king down there, and what if . . .

Yes, that was all good and sensible. But you can't always do What If. There are times when What If gets you precisely nowhere.

I jumped.

# 47

The bottom of the chamber came shooting up and I bent my knees ready but still the impact surprised me. Something gave way and for a second I was certain, absolutely certain, that I was plunging down into hell. Then the world steadied and I looked up and saw Daniel's head silhouetted against a segment of throbbing moon.

I didn't want to spend too long looking around. The pit smelled exactly how a hole bored deep into the cold earth should smell and that was OK, but the skeleton gave me the creeps now that I was up close to it. I didn't care if he'd once been Haxforth's brother, or king even of the whole wide world, I didn't want anything to do with him. I wasn't going to examine him in the name of *archaeology* or anything like that. And the silence down there. There was something terrifying about it, something eternal and not on the side of human beings.

I flicked the torch left and right. The dark patch I'd seen

from above wasn't really what I'd thought, wasn't much more than a scoop in the chamber wall, but it would do. There was enough space for a human body. No time to lose now. I looked up, waved my arm – tried to shout something – then all at once Haxforth's body came crashing down the shaft and earth was flying everywhere and I was trying to grab and steady him because it didn't seem right to just let him fall like a sack of potatoes. For a moment we did a death-dance in the narrow packed shaft, his face against mine like a cold grey flannel, then somehow I got him down below me, got him lying on the ground.

The earthfall stopped. It hadn't been so much after all. I waved up at Daniel to let him know I was all right. Carefully, carefully, I got Haxforth's body into the scooped-out part of the chamber, trying not to tread on the coins and armbands and all the other Historically Important bits and pieces that were lying around. Only I saw something then that made me forget Historically Important. Old Beautiful was down there too. It was nestled in behind the skull and its wings were rotten and there were some tiny white bones visible already. Its eyes though, they were still blackly alive and staring right at me. That and the burning tree when I first saw it, they're the two things I know I'll never be able to forget, images ripped from a nightmare, a cold knife pressed against my invincible heart.

I got myself back to the foot of the shaft, saw Daniel's head floating in the moonlight like a reflecting upside-down puddle. That was the way back to the real world. But I couldn't go up there yet. I waved again, made the beckoning bring-it-on motion with my hands. Daniel disappeared. A moment later the mail started coming down.

I don't know why, but I'd been expecting the bags, the

heavy black bags, to drop. And then for me to have to catch them or something. Daniel surprised me though. He was a surprising person in many ways when you got to know him. The mail came in tumbling handfuls instead, scoopfuls, individual items fluttering down. He must've seen the collapsing earth when Haxforth fell, must've realised the possibility of the walls caving in and decided to go about things the safe and thoughtful way.

I thought, Maybe I should try doing that myself sometime – in general ongoing life, I mean – if I ever get out of here.

Down it came, cascading over my shoulders and upturned head, piling round my feet. It was the sort of thing that you know if you ever saw it in a film there'd be big emotional music playing, perhaps even the sort of music Daniel played, and everything'd be slowed down and made out like it was some great life-changing moment. All that stuff I'd worried about for so long and now for it to be tumbling like snowflakes . . . truly poetic, you know? But it didn't feel that way at all. It was terrifying, being trapped in that cold forgotten place where the world and its rules felt distant and impossible.

I made a flat shovel of my two hands, started scooping the mail backwards into the dark spaces of the burial chamber. I threw it over Haxforth and Haxforth's brother and Old Beautiful, which if it wasn't dead by now soon would be. Behind me it all went, shovel and scoop, shovel and scoop, burying the old things and the old people. It kept coming. It didn't stop. For a while it was like I was standing at the bottom of some factory chute. All the recessed places were filled up and packed and after that I was standing on a mountain of paper rising steadily towards the moon. It wasn't too easy keeping a footing on that lot, it was all slip and slide, a quicksand of envelopes. I stamped it down hard with my boots though. I wasn't about to be sucked under, not now, no way.

'How much more?' I shouted up to Daniel after what seemed like hours.

I saw him put a hand behind his ear and shrug. Then saw an arm reach down into the hole, right up to the shoulder. At the end of the arm there was a leather loop for me to grab onto. Daniel's belt.

I leaped and felt the loop snap tight in my fist. I scrambled like a madman – found myself face down in a sea of frosted grass.

# 48

A clean-slicing wind had risen up from somewhere. It was time to go. The apple tree was half fallen over now. Nobody would give it a second glance, except maybe to think how the next good storm would topple it, bring it level with the crawling kingdom of insects and toadstools.

'That was a great idea, using the belt.'

'I did a life-saver's course once, at the swimming pool. They teach you stuff like that.'

Daniel was blue-lipped and wide-eyed and great shaking clouds of steam were coming out of his mouth, and I knew it couldn't all be from the cold.

'What was it like, down there? When I saw all that earth falling in on top I thought – well, I thought . . .'

'Come on,' I said. 'I'll tell you about it later.' There were still five or six bags lined up next to the mouth of the pit. Quickly we ripped them open, flung the contents in, down on hands and knees because that was faster. We watched the envelopes disappear into the earth. Finally the very last handful. I stood up. Daniel stood also, played his torch over the scene. Again I wondered whether I should say something. Haxforth was down there, after all, and his brother – though his brother'd been there an awful lot longer. Dust to dust, brothers together at last, thief and king. Rest in peace, you know, all that stuff.

I didn't say anything in the end. The dead can look after themselves, I figured. What I did instead was, as I dropped that final handful of mail, I made a wish for the living.

Don't ever expect me to tell you what it was though.

We gathered up the black plastic sacks, empty and ripped apart, and we crumpled them and threw those in too. Dropped the spade in on top. Then we heaved the two halves of the broken slab back into position. Neither of us said anything. Hastily we covered the stone with the piled-up mud and lumps of turf and climbed out of the valley. The moon was still big and bright and there was plenty of light to see by. Near the top, hunched in the sheltering edge of woodland, we turned and looked back. Right across the little sunken scar in the landscape, swathing the half-toppled apple tree, there lay a great wilderness of scrub and bramble.

You have never seen a more *anonymous* corner of the earth.

We turned and started to walk, me and Daniel. Heads down, hands thrust into pockets. Past the wreck of the van and across the farmer's field, searching for the place where Haxforth had crashed through the hedge. Somewhere an owl called and another called back. Out hunting. How long till seven o'clock? The police would be out hunting too, soon, ready to search our house and arrest Dad. I hoped to god he'd delivered the real-mail-that-mattered. Or at least had tried. Those Mitigating Circumstances needed to be in tip-top condition for the day when he'd have to stand up in court.

Three-quarters of the way across the field the tyre tracks we were following disappeared. New layers of frost were coming down, the air so cold it seemed to sparkle in front of your eyes. Underfoot the soil was hard as diamond, not a single imprint left of Christy's van's final wild ride. We doubled back, but now the *first* set of tracks were vanishing too. Suddenly the field seemed enormous. Before long all remaining energy was going into slogging ahead, trying to find a way out of that sub-zero world.

'If we keep walking in a straight line, we're bound to find a road or a house eventually,' Daniel said through shaking teeth.

You know the funniest thing? We'd opened up a hole in the ground and at the bottom there'd been GOLD. Real-life buried treasure – an Anglo-Saxon hoard. That gold would've made us rich and famous. Dad could've left Royal Mail, would never have had to work as a postman again. He'd've had time to look after Mum properly. And Daniel could've – well, I don't know what, but *something*, anyway. Yet neither of us even talked about it. Why? Of course we knew if the burial chamber ever came to be excavated all that mail would be found and then there'd be trouble. But it wasn't just that. Somehow we'd both known, without ever saying a word, that we hadn't gone there to take anything away. We were there to *leave* something, to finish a thing that had been going on for a long time, too long. And once that thing was finished Shuttle Hill would be closed up forever, like a fossilised flower bud. You couldn't ever open it again.

Once or twice as we trudged on I glanced at the figure shivering beside me and I knew he knew and understood all this.

Daniel Cushway was OK, when you came right down to it.

# 49

Barriers had been set up all along the top of Annandale Avenue. From the back of a flatbed lorry fluorescent-jacketed men lifted pickaxes, a hose, a big pneumatic drill. A couple of others were unhitching a grimy generator. Daniel and I stood watching them. The clear skies of the night had given way to grey cloud, the winter covering that's so familiar it feels like a second skin almost.

The men whistled and joked as they went about their work. One of them, passing close, saw us looking. 'Gas main's gone,' he said cheerily. 'Went overnight.'

We were back in town and it felt strange. I wasn't sure whether I liked it or not. For a while there in the darkness it'd felt like being trapped in an Ice Age. Only bit by bit had the twenty-first century seeped back. We found a track, and the track led to a path and the path led to gravel and tarmac and a place eventually where headlights whooshed past. A few minutes later an early-morning bus came cruising along, Out of Service the sign said but we flagged it down anyway. The driver let us on no problem, took one look, didn't even ask questions.

One of the fluorescent-jacketed men started up the generator. It coughed, vibrated, spewed oily smoke into the morning air. Another fiddled with the drill hose, a third passed around pairs of sky-blue ear defenders. The residents of Annandale Avenue were about to get an unpleasant surprise. Away we walked, not too fast, down the pavement towards number 79.

'What'll your mum say, you being out all night?' I asked Daniel.

'She'll go mental.' Then he realised what he'd said. 'I mean, she'll be really angry.'

'Tell her to get stuffed.'

'I can't do that,' he said miserably. 'I'm not brave enough.'

'You took on Christy, didn't you?'

'He got me down on the ground! I'd've been dead if it hadn't been for you.'

'But you were still *there*, that's what counted.'

He waved it away like it wasn't important at all.

We stood outside his house. 79 Annandale Avenue, with its perfect metal kitchen and all those books left behind by his dad. The driveway was empty and I heard the sigh of relief. Mrs Cushway must've been away at her court case again. Another early departure for Winchester. There'd probably be a million messages on Daniel's phone, whenever he turned it back on.

'Here,' Daniel mumbled. 'I think you'd better have this. It belongs to you, really.'

He dug around in his pocket and held out Haxforth's clasp.

That surprised me. I'd had this fleeting idea that he'd thrown it into the burial chamber back on Shuttle Hill, because somehow it seemed right to leave all the gold together. Now here it was, lying on the palm of his hand. The coiled hinge, the arrowhead catch. In a month, a year's time, it would be the only real proof that Haxforth ever existed.

Up the road, I saw the workmen pulling down their ear defenders.

I thought about all the things I'd seen and how lucky I was, having Daniel there to see them with me. I pushed his hand away. I'd made a promise about that clasp and people shouldn't ever break promises, not if they can help it.

'It's going to bring you good luck.' I don't know why I said that. It sounded like one of those meaningless things adults say when they can't think of anything real. But somehow I felt it was true.

'Do you think?'

'Definitely.'

All of a sudden the pneumatic drill ripped through the morning quiet, its metal point roaring and biting and the first lumps of tarmac lifting from the road's surface already. Faces appeared in windows up and down the Avenue.

'Wait a minute!' Daniel ran to his front door, fumbled with keys, went inside – was back out a moment later.

'Here.' He handed me something. 'This is yours.'

'Thanks. Only if it's OK . . .?'

We were both having to shout to make ourselves heard.

He nodded. 'See you around then?'

I looked at this place where he lived, Annandale Avenue, with its big houses and brand-new silver cars. There was no reason for me to come to this part of town any more, not without Dad's mail to deliver. I remembered as well the new school Daniel'd be going to, the out-of-town place with its old buildings and church-type thing and all the cricket pitches the size of aircraft runways.

'Sure,' I said. 'I'll see you around.'

I grabbed my bike. It was exactly where I'd left it, propped against the iron railings. It felt like days since I'd ridden it last, years since I'd stolen it on the night of meeting Haxforth. I wheeled it out to the pavement and Daniel waved at me from his front door and I waved back and then he went inside.

Where to now?

I could climb on that bike, the rusting racer, and go anywhere in the world. Anywhere. Go to places where nobody knew me or anything about me and I'd survive somehow, knowing a few tricks now like I did. And all the worry, all the guilt, all the bad things that lay in the past or were waiting ahead in the future, I'd leave all of that behind and I'd be free and I wouldn't leave a single footprint behind for anyone to follow.

Only, who was I kidding?

I had to go back, back home to Maresfield Crescent. Whatever was happening there, that's where I needed to be.

I shoved the heavy hardback inside my coat and pushed off. Behind me the road drill was screeching out shockwaves. I got up speed, headed for the quieter streets.

# 50

A couple of net curtains twitched in the house windows across the way. That'd be the neighbours, getting an eyeful. Probably they'd been watching since the moment the police first arrived. Disgusting, something like that happening on the Crescent, I imagined them saying. A man taken away in handcuffs – just like *Crimewatch*. Not that I gave a rat's arse about anything they ever thought or said. They didn't know the first thing about what'd really been going on.

There weren't any police in our house now. There wasn't anyone, or at least that was how it looked from outside. I turned in, pushing my old-new bike through the clicking closing gate. There were scuff marks on the front door but they were from where Dad had forced his way in yesterday night. Before going inside I took a peek at the back garden.

The shed door was flapping open. Inside I could see the high cobwebbed shelves with their old tins of paint and orange-flaked tools. They must have gone in there, the police and Royal Mail investigators, but I couldn't see any evidence of a proper search.

Evidence.

I took a deep breath and went into the house.

OK. Everything looked OK. Or, at least, the same. The kitchen was still foul with greasy water in the sink and the unwashed plates reeked and there was the red gas bill lying on the table like some ancient historical document. A halo of flies buzzed around the bin even though it was December and not really the time for flies.

I filled the kettle and clicked it to boil.

I drank a cup of water, waiting for it to boil.

I thought, I'm here, and the mail isn't, and the police aren't either and all those are good things and they can't be bad in any way.

I wondered where Dad was and what he was doing and I hoped he was all right.

I walked from room to room, looking at everything. Strange how I felt like an intruder, a thief, in my own house. Upstairs the sheets and blankets had been turned out of the airing cupboard and the wooden loft hatch lay broken in the bath. A few floorboards were up here and there, the ones that were loose already.

I thought how it must have been for them. It wasn't like they were searching for something small, a knife or a handgun or a memory stick. They were expecting to find mountains of mail. It should've been obvious, hitting them smack between the eyes. You can't hide mountains of mail under floorboards or in drawers.

I felt certain, by the time I'd gone round the whole house, that they'd given up fairly early on.

Back in the kitchen I made tea and stirred in some old powdered milk. The clock on the microwave said 08.54. The cloud outside had thinned and everything felt brighter so I opened some windows and a fresh chill began to travel through the house. I couldn't think about all the things that had happened the night before. My head was going to need plenty of processing time for that. I felt dead tired, like I hadn't slept in about ten years, but I didn't want to lie down and rest, knew somehow that I wouldn't be able to drop off even if I tried. So what I did was, I cleaned up the kitchen. I scooped the liquefying apple into the bin. I wiped down the table and I took a pair of rubber gloves out from under the sink and washed the dirty dishes with hot water from the kettle. Then I mopped the floor and threw out the bad food from the fridge, which was most of it, and I would've emptied the bin too only for that I needed a black bag and there weren't any so I had to leave it.

All the time knowing that the next visitor would decide the rest of my life.

Either it would be Dad.

Or it would be a social worker.

# 51

12.03. A key went into the lock and the door opened. Dad stood there, looking pale, like he was going to faint any minute.

'Jesus. Make me a cup of tea, would you, Aidan? Plenty of sugar.'

He gulped it down in one go then looked anxiously around. 'Good lad, you've had a clear-up.'

He was wearing the same clothes I'd seen him in last night. They were old and dirty then but they looked even worse now. The hair on his face was thicker, not stubble any more but the beginnings of a proper beard.

'They came. Just like you said they would.' He rubbed his face with the palms of his hands, rubbed it hard and groaned. 'Show me your elbow.'

He meant, Show me the place on your arm where I hurt you last night.

I rolled up the sleeve of my jumper and he looked at the

graze. It was small, about the size of a twenty-pence piece. It was scabbing over nicely. In a week or two it'd be gone.

'I shouldn't have done it. I'm sorry.'

'That's OK,' I said, because what did a graze matter after all.

We went into the lounge. The curtains were closed like they had been for weeks but before Dad sat down on the brown sofa he pulled them wide open. Bright winter light flooded the room.

'What did you do it with it, Aidan?'

'Do with what?'

'All the junk. You promised you wouldn't deliver it.'

'I didn't.'

'So where is it?'

'It's gone,' I said.

'Where?'

'Just – gone.' I didn't say anything more. I looked right at him, told him straight and direct with my eyes that he'd never find out, so better not ask again.

Silence. A *long* silence.

'I knew you knew,' he said sadly. 'About me hiding it in the shed.'

'But not that I was going out every morning doing your round.'

'No. I didn't know that. Take enough of those sleeping tablets and you wouldn't notice if the house was burning down. I've chucked them away, you'll be pleased to hear.'

'What happened, Dad? The police, the investigators – what happened?'

'Not much.' He stared at his shoes. 'They were expecting to find sackloads of mail, weren't they? But there wasn't anything. They had a good poke around. Even got me to open up the car. 'What have you done with it, what have you done with it?' they kept saying. And I said, "I've delivered it, like I'm paid to." Which wasn't *exactly* a lie . . .'

'You did it all?'

'Every last item. Grafted right through the night. What with that and everything else, it feels like I haven't slept in a month.'

By *everything else*, he meant Mum. I quaked inside, thinking about my visit to Tredegar House with Haxforth.

'But what did they say? About your job and having to go to court and all that?'

He squirmed around. 'There's been no mention of it. They released me without charge. Well, there wasn't any evidence, was there? No complaints either. Not one single one. That was another funny thing.'

Not *one single complaint*. And all those nights spent in alliance with the moon . . .

'It'd be nothing more than I deserve though,' he said. 'I've made such a mess of everything.'

'And Mum?' Feeling sick, knowing I couldn't put the question off any longer. 'Have you called them today? Talked to anyone there about, you know – what happened?'

'Look, Aidan, I'll tell you about that later. I'm all done in. I need to go upstairs, get my head down for a bit.'

I opened my mouth, wanting suddenly to shout at him for treating me like a child even after everything that'd happened. But I didn't. After the stunt I'd pulled yesterday I wasn't exactly in a position to go demanding things. At the top of the stairs he turned. There was a strange look on his face that I couldn't read. A look of concealment maybe. Was that all the future held for us then, just permanently hiding things from each other? And for us never to be the sort of people who did things openly and honestly?

'Wake me at four,' he said. 'It's important – four o'clock.'

I heard him go into the room he shared with Mum and shut the door and for a minute or two I heard him moving around and then there was quiet.

I went into the kitchen and stared out of the window. I wondered what I should do next. There was always something to do, something urgent, but now there wasn't. Now there was *nothing* to do.

Four o'clock. Perhaps Mum had stabilised and that's when we'd be going in to see her?

Or was that when we were due to be visited by social services? Pointed our way by the police? And that was the reason for the sly evasive look he'd given me from the top of the stairs?

I went up to my room, closed the door, sat on the bed. I knew I should try to get some sleep too but my brain wouldn't settle. From under my pillow where I'd put it I took out the heavy hardback Daniel had given me. For a while I just gazed at the gold lettering on the cover. Then, when I'd had enough of that, I opened it up. The inside front cover still said:

*Dennis Cushway, Berkeley, California.*
*May 1979.*

But I knew it belonged to me now.

The weird ancient runes on one side, the modern English on the other. I scanned the pages, turned to the back – thinking of what Miss Tuckett talked about in school, how storytellers always leave the best bits till last, even all those hundreds of years ago.

> *Now death held him fast,*
> *he had made his last use of lairs in the earth.*
> *Standing by him there were bowls and flagons,*
> *there were platters lying there, and precious swords,*
> *quite rusted through, as they had rested there*
> *a thousand winters in the womb of earth.*
> *And this gold of men was full of power,*
> *the huge inheritance, hedged about with a spell . . .*

Haxforth's curse. Living for all those centuries – could such a thing ever have happened? Was there really once a man like he'd described, a monster or magician, someone who could reach right into the pulse of life, turn it any way he wanted?

What I needed to do, I decided then, was to get everything down, everything that'd happened from beginning to end. And I needed to do it fast, or at least make a start, because a person could go off their head thinking about all those things from last night. So I hunted around for a pen and paper and I got writing. Sources, I thought. Miss Tuckett would be proud because now I understand why they're so important. Memories change, wishes or dreams get tangled up with them, and if a person isn't careful the things that really happened start getting mixed up with the things you only think happened, or even just wanted to happen.

But, I don't know, I guess I was pretty tired after all. I'd only written a page or two before my eyelids started sagging. I put the writing stuff aside. All that could wait for later. Really, there wasn't so much of a hurry.

I laid down and closed my eyes.

No moon. No collapsing paper houses. No Queen's head, fierce and full of punishment.

My sleep was deep and dreamless.

# 52

'Aidan! Aidan, come downstairs!'

'Huh?' I heard myself say. 'What?'

'Downstairs!'

I sat up not knowing where I was for a moment. Dad was standing in the open doorway. He was freshly shaved and washed and wearing a clean pair of trousers and a new shirt, one I hadn't seen before.

The red lights of the digital clock said 16.16.

Down below, I heard someone knocking at the front door.

'Who is it?' I said. They were knocking insistently, you could tell they weren't going to go away.

'Come down and answer the door. I want you to do it, Aidan.'

I followed down the stairs, him sliding ahead into the kitchen, and there on the table sat an enormous vase of pink and white flowers. In the frosted glass of the door I saw a figure raising its arm to knock.

'Who is it?' I whispered.

'Just answer the door.'

Suddenly I saw how nervous and tense he was.

Social worker?

Royal Mail investigators, with new evidence from somewhere?

I opened the door.

'Aidan Hale?'

A smartly dressed woman, mid-thirties. Blouse and jacket, rectangular glasses, straggly hair held up with a big tortoiseshell clip. Leather bag hanging from her shoulder.

Social worker.

'I'm Aidan,' I said quietly.

'Visitor for you.' The smartly dressed woman smiled and stood aside.

I leaned out of the door and looked down the passageway. There was another woman, hovering uncertainly by the gate.

Mum.

I ran out and kissed her and held her and kept kissing and holding her. 'Hello, Aidan,' she said. 'Hello.'

'May we come inside?'

I pushed the door wide and in they came. 'Everything spick and span,' the smartly dressed woman said, glancing around.

'Oh, that's how it is all the time,' I said. 'That's how we like it.'

'Excellent.'

I smiled and then Dad came forward with the pink and white flowers. He'd taken them out of the vase and water was dripping from the stems onto the carpet.

'Hello, Mary,' he said shyly.

'Hello, Bob,' said Mum.

'Nice to have you back.' There were wet silvery points around the rims of his eyes.

Mum took the flowers, lifted them to her nose, laid them carefully on the kitchen table. Her head moved this way and that, taking everything in.

Dad sat down at the table and so did the smartly dressed woman. It seemed like they'd met before. I filled the kettle and clicked it to boil, not knowing what else to do but remembering something I'd heard once, about social workers and how much power they have.

Mum stayed on her feet, still hovering. You could tell she didn't know what to do next.

'You're well trained, Aidan,' the social worker said. 'I'll help you make the tea, if you like.'

'All right,' I said.

'I've heard a lot about you, from your mum. In fact I feel like I know you already. I'm afraid you're going to be seeing rather a lot of me in the coming weeks.' She took an ID card from an inside pocket of her jacket and held it out to me. Her first name was Hannah or Harriet or something, but she didn't hold the card up long enough for me to read it properly. It started with an H anyway.

'Yesterday's incident was extremely unfortunate. Nobody really seems to understand what happened. A bird getting into the room like that – it'd upset anyone if you ask me, let alone someone who's had to spend time at Tredegar House. But, well – overall – we don't think it's helping your mum at the moment, being there. Sometimes places like that can hold up a recovery as much as help it. It's commonly recognised. The doctors think that what she really needs is to be back at home with the people she knows and loves. That doesn't mean she's completely better though, or that she won't ever have to go back. It's important you understand that, Aidan.'

'I understand.'

'Just like it's important that you need to take really good care of her, now she's home. Do you think you can do that?'

I nodded. 'I'll try my best.'

'I'm sure you will.'

The social worker lifted her leather bag onto the kitchen table, started taking out forms that were green and yellow and white. 'It's funny sometimes what a change of environment can do. We'd told her she was coming home but, you know, it was like she didn't really realise it until this morning. And then you perked up almost immediately, didn't you, Mary?'

Mum didn't say anything. She was watching the kettle tremble on its white plastic base, watching the wild boiling bubbles as they clung to the inside of the see-through panel on the side. Then the cut-off switch kicked in and the kettle fell silent, and the kitchen too.

The social worker made to stand up, to help.

'Aidan'll do it,' Dad said. 'He knows where everything lives.'

'If you don't mind?' the social worker asked.

'No, I don't mind.'

There was fresh milk in the fridge when I looked and things in the cupboards too where the shelves had been empty before. I made tea in a teapot, carried it over to the table together with our best cups and a bowl of sugar. Nobody spoke while I did it but it wasn't one of those silences that's uncomfortable. On a plate I laid out some custard creams, arranged them carefully in a fan shape. I don't know why, it just seemed the right thing to do.

'Of course,' the social worker said, 'it's mainly down to the medication. Finding out what works best together. It's vitally important Mary keeps up with her regime, that goes without saying. What we need now is a period of stability. There's a supply here, and you can get more from your GP when you run out. There's various things I need to go through with you, Mr Hale, and some documents you'll need to sign . . .'

'Aidan,' said Dad, 'take your mum out into the garden for a minute, will you?'

I held Mum's hand and led her outside to the green square of lawn with its borders of winter-sleeping plants and its ordinary garden shed. The sky was clear and blue, fading to purple already in one vast corner. An hour from now it would be dark and the moon coming around. But none of that mattered any more.

Steam poured from our mouths as we stood there looking at each other.

'How do you feel, Mum?'

'Tired,' she whispered. 'But different. Peaceful.'

'I'll make sure you take everything. All the pills and stuff. That's my job from now on. To look after you.'

She smiled and touched my shoulder. Blonde hair, overweight in her grey cardigan and tracksuit bottoms. Beautiful. I thought of the photograph of us eating ice creams on the beach. How her eyes in that picture were clear and free of confusion. How they looked the same now.

'Everything's so quiet,' she said. 'I'd forgotten.'

She was right. I listened to the silence. There were no cars, no TVs, no neighbours. Just our invincible hearts pushing us on through the bare branches of an English winter. It must have been like this in the year when Haxforth's brother was crowned, or when the man who wrote *Beowulf* first picked up his pen.

'It's the blue sky,' said Mum. 'Now there's the same silence in here, too.' She tapped the top of her head.

'No voices?'

'Not today.'

I heard the gate go. The social worker was leaving. I knew she'd be back, tomorrow or the day after. But that was OK because somehow I didn't feel afraid any more about all those tomorrows.

Dad came outside. And all we did then was hold onto each other, the three of us, hold on really tight.

Blue skies forever.

# BONE JACK

## SARA CROWE

Ash's dad has returned from war. He's close to a breakdown, lost in a world of imaginary threats. Meanwhile, Ash's best friend Mark is grieving and has drifted away into his own nightmares. Ash's only escape is his lonely mountain running, training to be the stag boy in the annual Stag Chase.

But dark things are stirring. Ghostly hound boys prowl the high paths, and in the shadows a wild man watches. Could Mark and Dad be haunted by more than just their pasts?

'Dark, magical, and mysterious, *Bone Jack* captured me and carried me away'
*Rebecca Stead*

9781783440054 £6.99

# The Cry of the Wolf

# MELVIN BURGESS

'A writer of the highest quality with exceptional powers of insight.'
*Sunday Times*

It was a mistake for Ben to tell the Hunter that there are still wolves in Surrey. For the Hunter is a fanatic, always on the lookout for unusual prey. Driven by an ambition to wipe out the last English wolves, the Hunter sets out on a savage quest. But what happens when the Hunter becomes the hunted?

'A disturbing book, but of real quality; you will applaud the end.'
*Observer*

'A Dickens of the future.'
*Michael Rosen*

9781849393751 £6.99

# BLOODTIDE

# MELVIN BURGESS

'An epic tale of treachery, deceit, sex, torture, violence, revenge and retribution' *Independent on Sunday*

*'Love. Hate. So what? This is family. This is business.'*

London is in ruins. The once-glorious city is now a gated wasteland cut off from the rest of the country and in the hands of two warring families – the Volsons and the Connors.

Val Volson offers the hand of his young daughter, Signy, to Connor as a truce. At first the marriage seems to have been blessed by the gods, but betrayal and deceit are never far away in this violent world, and the lives of both families are soon to be changed for ever . . .

'Shies from nothing, making it both cruel and magnificent' *Guardian*

9781849396950 £6.99